I0603827

TRAVELS INTO THE BREACH

Accounts of a Reclusive Mystic

Evelyn Klebert

Dedication

For E.M.P.

Who taught me through her fire, fierceness, and strength how to walk the road less traveled.

Table of Contents

TRAVELS INTO THE BREACH

Accounts of a Reclusive Mystic

The Three

"There are three of them."

"Really? Are you quite sure?"

"Yes," she frowned succinctly as though it were something she often did — too often, he imagined.

"Go on." He was taking notes, not extensive notes, just impressions as they crossed his mind, things that he might want to return to later.

"I suppose it sounds ridiculous, but it feels like they are attacking me."

He stopped and glanced up. They were sitting on the screen porch at the back of his wood-frame house on the corner of Moss St. and St. John Court. "What makes you think that?"

"I, well, have dreams, and I feel things," she hesitated. "Mostly fatigue lately, so tired that I can't think. I had the doctor run some tests, but they can't find anything."

He'd stopped taking notes altogether now and leaned back in the wicker rocking chair, staring for a moment at her. It was more than true that the colors around her were turbulent — brown, yellow, orange, and disturbingly ugly splotches of red here and there — the telltale signs of an attack, a psychic attack.

"The three, have you narrowed it down, who they are?"

She shifted a bit nervously as though the very question gave her discomfort. She was tired. He could feel that emanating from her easily, and there was pain here — emotional and spiritual.

"I believe so," she said quickly and then turned away, staring at the view of Bayou St. John outside his screen porch.

"If I'm truly going to be able to help you at all, Mrs. Ellerman, then it's important to be candid with me."

She turned to him with intensity in her soft brown eyes. At that moment, it struck him how difficult and personal this was for her. "Mr. McKellan, you have to understand that even the fact that I have someone willing to honestly listen to me is more than astounding."

Now it was his turn to frown. "Mrs. Ellerman, you must believe me that I take these matters very seriously."

"I do believe you, Mr. McKellan. I have read more than one of your books, so I know that you are an expert of esoteric philosophy, of parapsychology."

"There's something that you are afraid to say, Mrs. Ellerman." This was more than clear. It was written all over her, and more than that, he could sense it profoundly in her emotions. She was painfully torn by some sort of obligation.

"Yes, well, one of the three is Lydia Dressel. She manages a gift shop in the French Quarter. Another is a woman named Jocelyn Accuro. She is a manicurist and works in Mid-City."

He waited but recognized that Irena Ellerman was not going to continue without his prodding. "And the third, Mrs. Ellerman?"

That frown, again, it was unfortunate. Otherwise, she would have been an attractive woman, but a perpetual dour expression eventually tends to seep into one's soul, soaking and permeating all otherwise happy crevices.

"The third Mr. McKellan, unfortunately, is my very own cousin Annabelle, someone who at one time was as close to me as a sister."

Annabelle Killian, as it was, had once been married, now divorced. Irena Ellerman herself was also married, and happily, she professed, though Malachi had to admit she did not look happy. But then again, when an ugly insect invades your pristine garden over time, all you can seem to focus on is how to expunge the intruder. And in this case, it was a relative, one who had certain keys to one's inner life. Of course, the keys could be withdrawn, and in his personal opinion, more often than not should be.

He'd given her tea, the young Mrs. Ellerman, still in her thirties, he assessed. It was a sort of mint tea blended with chamomile. He found it soothing, and Irena Ellerman did need soothing.

"So, how did you come to this conclusion about this particular cluster of women?"

"Well, they are all friends. Their pictures are always up together on the networks."

"Networks?"

"Yes, you know Facebook, Instagram — those are the only two I participate in."

Malachi himself was a 64-year-old, somewhat reclusive author who did these sorts of little investigative forays as a side interest. For him, social networks actually weren't a place he spent any time.

"I see, but the attacks?"

She nodded, "Yes, well, one of them, one of the women, is a self-professed witch. You know the spells and all that business."

"Well, on its face, that might not be so much of a problem. There is a large community of many well-intentioned white witches, and Wiccans committed to doing good."

"Yes, I know. I don't want you to think that is what has brought me to this conclusion. I — I began retrieving things around my house after she visited."

"She?"

"My cousin Annabelle, she would leave things around, hidden things in my house — jewelry, hair pins, strange dried herbs sometimes. Then as I began to pay attention, I noticed other things of mine would turn up missing, a shirt, a scarf, and even more personal items."

"Such as?"

Again, she moved about nervously, and Malachi knew what was coming. These people were never particularly imaginative. "A bra and then underwear."

He sighed deeply, "And you're sure you didn't simply misplace them?"

"Yes, I do keep track, oddly enough. I knew it was her, the timing of it all. What could they be doing with my things?"

"And the cousin, what does she do?"

"Teaches mathematics at a University."

"Doesn't seem like such an activity for a level-headed mathematics professor."

"Hard to say. She's always seemed unhappy to me, and unhappy people sometimes go to great lengths to assuage their pain."

He nodded at her astute estimation. "True enough."

They were in the cottage, actually a mountainside cottage, seated in front of a roaring fireplace on a very chilly day. The season exactly couldn't really be pinpointed. But it wasn't spring, possibly late November, late November, sometime in a lovely, undefined mountain range.

Simon Tull smoked his pipe and paced across the shiny pine wood floor in the den. He was a young, brown-skinned English gent in his late twenties who occasionally slipped into a cockney accent when over-excited. He also happened to be Malachi's spirit guide. According to Simon, they'd had many former life connections, and the cottage, well, that was Malachi's creation through visualization. And the pretty cocker spaniel sitting on one end of his very comfortable suede, dark tan couch was Nuance — a dog from his childhood, this lifetime, which tended to drop in on his subconscious whenever it suited her.

"Hmm," Simon continued to pace. He'd always been a bit of a high-strung type. "Was there animosity between these cousins to cause the Killian woman to launch such an attack?"

"Nothing overt, according to Irena, just perhaps some latent jealousy of her cousin's successful marriage."

"What about the other two?"

"Ah yes, the dark witch and the manicurist. Not really sure, except just driving near the French Quarter shop where Lydia Dressel works, there is quite a strong residue of the black arts. No matter how benign she professes to be, she has been dabbling on the wrong side of the tracks." Simon paused, placing his long dark cherry wood pipe in the ashtray atop the redwood mantel of the fireplace. "You know, if you were still in the flesh, I'd certainly harangue you about your smoking."

"It's one of my very few indulgences. Do you want me to help you with the book tonight?"

"No, I'd rather try to figure out how to help young Mrs. Ellerman."

"You know, you're not that old yourself, Malachi."

"Oh, at times, I have to admit, I feel absolutely ancient."

He didn't want to meet them, the three in the flesh. In truth, there didn't seem to be all that much point to it. So instead, he focused on them one by one. The first was the unknown — the manicurist, Jocelyn Accuro.

What he needed was a picture, an image, to concentrate on, and in the social media-hungry generation, what he needed was pretty easy to obtain with a quick computer search. There she was in all her glory, one Jocelyn Accuro. She was what he'd call an interesting-looking woman — large dark eyes, rather tanned skin, and a shade of red hair that he was more than sure could not be natural.

Running off the image on his color printer, Malachi retired to a quiet room in the center of his home. The furnishings within were sparse, with some large throw pillows on the floor and a very plush but sedate Oriental rug in soothing tones of blue and gray.

For him, it was a working room, a place of meditation. Malachi McKellan considered himself, amongst many things, to be a detective of sorts — a detective of the paranormal who only took on those particular cases that spoke to him.

He placed the picture on the floor before him, removing his shoes and settling into a comfortable cross-legged position.

Breathing in and out, he somewhat carefully measured his breaths for a few moments, then closed his eyes. Near him were a few substantial chunks of unpolished quartz crystals and several pillar-sized white candles he'd lit. He calmed himself, retaining focus on his goal, allowing himself to sink into another level of consciousness. Just in the moments before he felt his spirit leave his body, he could succinctly hear Simon's voice somewhere near him. "Mind if I tag along?"

"Of course, you're always welcome."

Traveling through the astral plane was always exceedingly different from taking a stroll down the street. Movement is precipitated by thought, and the physical eyes give way to a different sort of vision or perception, if you will. It is ostensibly seeing but often feeling a bit out of the frame of regular physical vision.

"What is this place?"

"Place of work, I'd imagine." Simon was beside him, but they communicated solely by thought-form. It had taken Malachi years, actually decades, to master pure thought communication. One had to work hard to rein in the mind and distill extraneous clutter from the process.

The long pale blue room was filled with people, customers, nail technicians, pedicurists, and, unfortunately other things.

"This certainly is a difficult place."

"So much human traffic in and out. The people, they're bound to bring things with them."

He and Simon slowly moved more deeply within. The vivid colors swirled around them, energy frenetically flying off people, chaotic rhythms of loud sound, and then of course, the creatures. People really had no idea of the weird train of interdimensional creatures that follow them around. They were not unlike varying flocks of birds and squirrels that might follow you in a park, desperate for some morsel of food.

But here, it was different. These creatures fed on energy, every morsel that is carelessly spilled by humans. There were all sorts of creatures — some flying, some dragging around partially on incomplete limbs, and some as flat as pancakes flipping about like some sort of amoeba entities.

Some were benign, but others were actively parasites, attacking people and digging in on wounded spots. As he and Simon stood quietly in the middle of the active room, they watched. Malachi noted one woman having her nails done absolutely covered in flat disk-like creatures about the size of a potholder, quivering jellyfish-like things. "How does she stand it?" he murmured.

Simon took in the sight with little reaction. "One gets accustomed to it, I suppose. Not even cognizant of the irritation after a while."

And then, looking away with a measure of disgust, Malachi noted their target walking with purpose across the room.

"Try to focus on why we're here. Remember, collecting information."

Malachi zeroed in on the figure now sitting at a table across from an elderly woman. He estimated Jocelyn Accuro to be in her forties, with dark red hair in a loose bun at the back of her head. There was activity — strange fluttering things around them both, but there was entirely too much going on here, too much to isolate what was connected to whom.

"Malachi, what is it?"

"It's too difficult, too much extraneous interruption."

"Yes, of course, perhaps if we traveled backward."

Malachi again focused intensely on Jocelyn Accuro, concentrating, seeing her momentarily affixed in time. Then in his mind, because thought on this plane quickly transmuted into reality, he was able to place her back. He envisioned her back further to the morning, then early morning, then the night before, asleep in her bed.

"Yes, that's best, in isolation."

And as if in agreement, their environment collapsed inward in a fluttering moment, something akin to cake batter that folded in on itself, then settled into a new coherence.

In a shifting, disorienting instant, things became recognizable again. They were in a room, a rather long bedroom with a set of French doors on one side leading to a patio. Directly over the bed was a brass ceiling fan complementing the queen-size brass bed that Jocelyn lay in. The dark red satin bedspread contrasted sharply against an espresso furniture set.

"Bold choices," murmured Simon.

Malachi looked around, trying to focus, and then he began to see the fluttering all across the headboard, the bedspread, the furniture. It was like a thousand tiny moths that blended into anything they landed on. Until, of course, they moved and reflected an ugly iridescent shade of orange.

Malachi sighed wearily. He'd seen it before.

"Residue," Simon mumbled.

"Seem so," Malachi answered.

"I thought the other one was the dark witch."

"That's what Irena Ellerman said, but I'm more than sure she has no real idea what's happening. Miss Accuro is clearly taking an active hand in these ritualistic attacks against Irena. It would be extraordinarily advisable if, before one engages in these activities, they understood the real consequences of what they are doing."

In the bed, the body of Jocelyn Accuro shifted, and with her, a wave of parasitical moths fluttered upward momentarily.

"Byproducts are always created in these sorts of ceremonies. Things that want to feed and attach themselves to the first living energy they can find."

"What do you think they've been up to exactly?" Simon asked though Malachi had the distinct impression that he already knew the answer. Simon had always taken his role as spirit guide, and all that implied very seriously. As far as he was concerned, he was a mentor to Malachi.

"Well, if it were positive, our little friends wouldn't exist. I'm sure it amounts to stealing energy, given Irena Ellerman's state of depletion. How very foolhardy, though. What little they gain, they lose by making themselves more vulnerable to the parasites of this world and, of course, the ones they create."

"Are you ready to leave?" Simon asked.

"In a moment, I think I'd like to check just one more thing."

Malachi cleared his mind and focused even more deeply. He focused on the spirit, the ethereal essence of Jocelyn Accuro. For him, it truly wasn't a matter of judgment. If he were to take it upon himself to sit in judgment upon the souls of this earth who chose to clothe themselves so perilously in human flesh, then he would be unable to obtain the skills needed truly to be of assistance. After all, everyone ultimately incarnates to learn, to evolve, and one of the best teachers was one's mistakes.

He paused. It was as he thought. What they were looking at was actually just a body. She was traveling in her dream state, and the parasitic moths were just continuing to feed off the spiritual energy that still remained with the flesh.

"I'm following her," he murmured to Simon, having taken off before he ever heard a reply.

The dream state is a complicated business. Within it, one could travel through and access many different dimensions, realities, and levels of consciousness. Though if one was genuinely unaware, as most tended to be, it could end up being an exhausting and sometimes barbaric venture.

He stopped, stopped short. It took a moment, but once he got his bearings, he found himself stepping through a curious, messy muck.

"You could've waited, old boy, until I caught up."

"Sorry, but I knew you'd get here eventually if we could figure out precisely where this is."

Simon seemed to be taking it all in a bit distastefully. "Feels like something of a nightmare, wouldn't you say?"

Malachi attempted to absorb the dreariness of their surroundings. Outside of the sludgy muck on the floor that they seemed to be sloshing through, there was also a tangibly molding quality to the structure around them. Pulsating dingy green patches covered the walls and the nearly claustrophobically low ceiling. At first glance, it appeared to be some sort of old wooden building, possibly rural. Scurrying and scrambling across the furniture and even the pictures on the walls were rodents and roach-like bugs.

Mwumm, mwumm, mwumm — in the distance, somewhere not far, he could hear it, some sort of relentless chanting — *mwumm, mwumm.*

He waded with difficulty, pushing through the slop and passed through an arched doorway into another room. Candles lighted this one, black candles it seemed, illuminating the dingy interior.

His head spun from the noxious stench permeating the space. He knew it was all just like the moths, a byproduct of the negative energy being produced. In the center, he was less surprised than dismayed to find the women — the three in question, all completely naked and having etched garish symbols on themselves in what could only be construed as blood.

He stilled his natural reaction of gripping nausea at the disturbing vision so that he could think. In the center was one with long black hair, and the other two holding one arm as they chanted. The woman being held had her eyes closed. But it continued to sicken him as he felt what was happening. Jocelyn and the other — Lydia Dressel, he believed — were actually actively draining the spiritual energy out of who he now assumed was Annabelle Killian, draining her down to critical levels. And she, in her ignorance, had no idea.

Adele Blanchard brought two strong cups of *Espresso Stop's* praline coffee to the front door of Malachi McKellan's residence. She'd called him about midmorning several times to no avail. She supposed she should have waited for him to call her back but felt something was off, so she persevered.

She and Malachi had been acquaintances for around five years and more closely in the last three. Malachi was a widower who'd lived alone for over a decade, and Adele was divorced, twice in fact, and owned one of the few surviving metaphysical bookshops in New Orleans.

That was how they met. Malachi was something of a celebrity in his field, although he endeavored, and rather strenuously so she thought, to keep a low profile. Adele had always considered him one of the city's well-hidden treasures. Three sharp knocks on the front door, and then she waited, though she wouldn't wait long. Patience was a quality she had never cultivated. She tapped her feet a bit nervously. It was a lovely April day and somewhat curiously on the chilly side. She hadn't worn a sweater — damned unpredictable weather.

She lifted her hand for one more sharp knock when the door abruptly swung open.

She smiled with retail animation. "I thought you'd gone back to sleep."

He did not return her smile. His well-clipped white and black mottled beard looked slightly unkempt this morning. She was right. Something must be off.

"Adele, it's not the best —"

"But I brought you a coffee. Surely, you won't refuse a visit from a well-meaning friend."

He stared at her with that discriminating stare that made her feel as though he was peering right into her core. "No, apparently I won't," he said with the slightest measure of irritability and then opened the door just wide enough for her to cross the threshold.

"I was torn about the Ellerman girl, whether or not I should refer her to you." Adele Blanchard was direct. On top of that, she was rather psychic in her own right or perhaps just bursting with feminine intuition, which for all intents and purposes meant that she was very psychic.

"So, you said," he murmured. They sat in his den, he sipping the overly sweet coffee that Adele had bestowed on him. He watched as she paced in front of his fireplace, which, as it was in this climate, rarely got lit.

"Yes, I suppose I did when I asked if you would consider seeing her. There was something desperate about the little thing, and Annette, you know my palmist, thought outside forces were working against her."

"Yes, well, Annette is very astute."

"Yes, she's a jewel. I'm so lucky to have found her. So, have you seen her?"

Another sip, actually the sugar was helping his completely depleted energy. "Yes, I did yesterday."

She'd stopped moving.

Adele was rather a striking woman. In her early fifties — honey blonde hair pulled back always in a bun, an exotic-looking shawl draped over a black knit dress. Though he had to admit, the frenetic energy she exuded sometimes felt exhausting. "You did? And how did that go?"

Good question. It all felt like a bit of a muddle just now. "Ongoing. I'm not sure exactly what I can do for her at this point."

"Well, Malachi, if anyone can, it's you."

He smiled grimly. She'd settled down on the moss-green sofa next to him. "You seem so tired. Are you all right?"

He patted her hand absently. She really was a lovely woman and would have made an excellent companion, he thought, in his later years. But something had always stopped him — a knowledge that somehow that would not be their path together.

"Answer me something, Adele."

"Anything."

"Why do women turn on each other, women who should be family?"

"That? Well, there are all sorts of reasons, I suppose. Betrayal perhaps or just perceived betrayal, competition, unfortunately, we often feel pitted against each other or jealousy. That's a big one."

"A toxic business."

"Yes, I've always thought men have the brawn, but women can have a level of venom that cannot be matched."

"So, at present, Annabelle Killian appears to be some sort of victim in this matter." Simon was pacing in front of the smoldering fireplace in Malachi's mind-created cottage. It was chilly. He wondered absently why it was always a bit chilly here, given that they were traipsing about some level of his subconscious mind. Perhaps, it was a backlash to the inordinately hot, muggy weather he lived with in New Orleans.

"Victim? Perhaps, at least in Jocelyn Accuro's dream, she appeared to be the one being drained of energy by the other two—"

"Witches?"

"I don't like the term myself. It's been appropriated to have such negative connotations these days."

"It's true. In the old days, they were positive forces — healers, practitioners of white magic. This tawdry business, well, it's an aberration."

It struck him as odd, the contradictions that came from his old friend Simon Tull. On the surface, he was dressed as a turn-of-the-century young man of color in his early twenties. But the wisdom from him felt undeniably like a much older soul and mentor, well-seasoned by many lifetimes and with knowledge far beyond the years that his youthful appearance suggested.

"But she is the link to Irena Ellerman. She is her cousin. She has had access to her home, her things. And I have noticed evidence of severe draining in Irena's aura."

Simon stopped pacing, settling in the overstuffed club chair near the fireplace. It was more than true that if this place were actually physical, Malachi would move in permanently. "So now we need to focus on Annabelle Killian and try to sort out her role in this."

"Yes, I suppose so," Malachi answered, still feeling the fatigue of their last excursion.

"Perhaps, you should wait a bit, old friend, and recharge first. You do seem tired."

"No, no, I intend to take a nice long rest once this business is settled."

And so, he began the process of focusing intently on the image of Annabelle Killian. There was no need for a picture. Her face from Jocelyn Accuro's dream was quite distinctly etched in his mind. The last thing he remembered before he moved on was Nuance rubbing up against his feet as she always used to do when he was a boy.

He hadn't focused on a particular place, just allowed the strongest impressions of Annabelle to draw him. The environment felt fluid, transient in some respects. But eventually, it solidified, and he found himself in one-half of a double in the Lakeview area of New Orleans. The house itself was a wood frame, not unlike a shotgun construction. He was standing directly in front of a den with a short sofa, several chairs, and a sort of disembodied, oddly placed brick chimney in the center. Just beyond was a kitchen and a small breakfast table at the back. Strangely at the moment, the house seemed serene, and the woman in question sat at a round table silently typing on her laptop computer.

"That's very odd," Simon commented beside him. "Much less dramatic than Jocelyn Accuro's place."

"Yes," Malachi moved a bit closer to the woman steadily working on her computer. The atmosphere directly around her was perplexingly discordant with the rest of the house. "Someone or something must be trying to help her."

"Yes, perhaps you're right."

Malachi moved around the house, trying to feel, trying to sink deeper to understand what indeed was happening here. The woman at the table felt frantic, disorganized, and, more than anything, confused. He sank even deeper into awareness, simply staring at her or rather her aura, what was left of it as it was greatly diminished. No wonder she couldn't think. Clearly, she was almost completely drained of energy.

Again, in the blink of an eye, Simon was beside him. "I found evidence of light workers here, sending her energy, trying to steer her toward her path. She is meant to help people, Malachi, but these associations have completely drawn her off course."

"With the witches," he murmured.

"With the dark witches," Simon answered.

"We should see the other one — the Dressel woman. It might help illuminate what is happening here."

Malachi shifted course, focusing deeply on the essence of Lydia Dressel. It pained him to do so. Acutely, he could feel a loss of energy through his heart chakra. So was the case when one actively chose to brush near those enmeshed by darkness.

This one was the practitioner. Jocelyn Accuro might well be the most naturally powerful drainer of energy, but Lydia Dressel, with her long chestnut brown, permed hair, was the architect — and, of course, the ego behind the victimization of Irena Ellerman and her cousin Annabelle Killian.

Malachi wasn't the least surprised that focusing on Lydia Dressel brought him back to the horrific wood frame, country house that had appeared so nightmarishly in Jocelyn Accuro's dream. It was the center of too many dark ceremonies. These ceremonies had given birth to the infestation of parasites that he had seen literally covering Jocelyn's body and invading what he now concluded was the country home of Lydia Dressel.

He stood in the center of her den, which appeared somewhat normal at the offset, not filled with the murky swamp or walls crawling with hungry, aberrant creatures waiting for unexpected prey to pounce upon.

But he didn't have to see it to feel it.

"What a waste," Simon murmured. "Clearly, the woman has gifts but directs them towards selfish purposes."

"She's damaged herself, Jocelyn Accuro, and most likely Annabelle Killian."

He felt the draw upstairs, a distinct pull, and within a moment, he was there. Lydia Dressel was sitting on an antique cherry wood, four-poster bed, crouched over a book, reading to herself. Her lips moved, murmuring while she dropped various ingredients into a dish.

"Herbs of some sort," Simon whispered with a bit of disdain in his voice. "Skin of some unfortunate animal as well as innards and blood, I believe, hers and its."

"Barbaric," Malachi muttered.

But this was not what he wanted to see. He already knew the woman engaged in all sorts of unsavory activities. Inwardly, he shifted his focus. The room fluttered around them for a moment as though it dipped in and out of vision, then returned to daytime with Lydia Dressel still sitting on the bed, but now with Annabelle Killian seated beside her.

Lydia spoke in a rather high-pitched tone that grated a bit on Malachi's nerves. Then again, he held a natural revulsion toward the woman.

"Thank you, Anna, so much for letting me have this bed. Its energy is wonderful."

The other woman smiled, seeming hungry for validation. "Of course, I wasn't using it. It belonged to my great Aunt."

Malachi focused on the cherry wood headboard behind them and the four posters surrounding them. "The original owner, she was a practitioner as well," he murmured.

"Yes, yes, I can see it too — a dark practitioner and angry, so angry at that family who took her things."

"Took her possessions, you mean?" Malachi asked.

"Indeed, she believes they were stolen. The energy of this bed is powerfully toxic, and this woman, Lydia Dressel, is using it to control the Killian woman, inflaming her emotions."

Simon shook his head. "It's such a base energy. She's using such a low frequency."

The deep red headboard of the bed behind them formed a massive semicircle not too far from the low ceiling in the room. It was covered with a minimal flourish, just an inlay of the same wood outlining beneath the curve. But just staring at it for moments, he could see the ugly red film of energy oozing from its crevices, so thick it was like a gel streaming from hidden cracks, dripping down the wood.

"How could anyone bear to sleep in it at all?" Simon muttered.

"Even negativity can be perceived as power by some. It influences, influences the baser instincts, the uninvolved emotions — triggers anger, hate, jealousy, and fear — mostly and always fear. But this is only a tool. There must be more."

"Did you get what I asked?" Lydia Dressel directed to her companion.

Annabelle nodded, "I did, but it felt strange just taking her things."

Lydia, stretching a welcoming smile on her sharply boned face, made Malachi cringe inwardly. "It's all about balance, achieving balance, Annabelle. I'm just trying to help you. Irena has been given so much, too much, and you unfairly overlooked. I was brought into your life to help you, guide you."

"I know, and I am grateful."

"Then don't worry. We won't be hurting Irena a bit, just helping to give you more energy."

Annabelle nodded. Malachi could feel her indecision. She was suppressing her feelings. She knew there was something wrong, but she doubted herself. And she was hungry, starving in fact, for validation, attention, for what her cousin had or what she perceived — love and happiness.

"How clever she is," Simon commented dryly. "She knows just what to say, what buttons to push, to get her to do what she wants."

"Yes, but that doesn't exempt Annabelle Killian from the consequences of her actions."

"The light workers are trying to help her."

"Indeed," Malachi murmured. "But the more she damages her spirit in the Dressel woman's ceremonies, the less they will be able to protect her."

Malachi went home. There was always a choice to be made — to help or to allow people to follow their own paths. He sat on his porch, watching the evening sun slowly slip out of view into the cool waters of the Bayou St. John. Though, of course, it was simply an optical illusion. If the sun actually sunk into its waters, they would be on fire, boiling, and the world on fire as well.

He thought about his late wife, Josie as he often did in the quiet moments. He wondered what she would say in this circumstance. Probably *"Malachi, do the best you can do to save them all. Then when you've done everything you can, let it go — all of it."* Sometimes it was torture to be here without her, and he could barely wait for the day they would be together again. But then he reminded himself that he was indeed here for some reason — still here. There was work to be done, and he had promised Irena Ellerman that he would try to help her. Unfortunately, unraveling and sorting out this sticky web would indeed be part of the process.

He was tired. Malachi took the morning off walking around the perimeter of Bayou St. John and across its great metal walking bridge to the other side.

The air was crisp, just bordering on chilly but would quickly heat up as the day proceeded. He put the case firmly out of his mind, just for now. Oftentimes, he found that it was best to step away from things, then later return with a fresh perspective.

It was relatively early, just approaching seven now, so the normal foot traffic, people jogging, walking their dogs, hadn't started in full force yet. It was soothing being out near the water. It was a very old area, first populated by American Indians and after those early European settlers, some even before the city of New Orleans proper — or rather the French Quarter — was colonized. People, as a necessity and in an elemental way, had always been drawn to the water. The water was a conductor of energy, and unbeknownst to most, energy was as much a dire component of living as food or water. People were not simply this physical shell, this flesh with no connection to the divine. When God created in his image, that image was spirit, spirit that had to be protected and nurtured as much or perhaps more than taking care of a physical body as is done with exercise and a healthy lifestyle.

He breathed in deeply the cool air. When indeed did the spirit become buried and forgotten under the loud roar of civilization building? The kingdom is within. It has always been so.

He stopped on the metal bridge midway, staring out across the water. This was the problem in a nutshell. These women, particularly Lydia Dressel and Jocelyn Accuro, understood that there is power in the spiritual realm and understood the need and power in acquiring energy. So, they were using ceremonies, in some ways barbaric ceremonies, to acquire it. The problem is the same as children wielding machine guns. There is so little knowledge that they do not understand the spectrum of ramifications of their actions — the damage not only to Irena Ellerman and Annabelle Killian but to themselves and any other bystanders caught up in their collateral damage. He sighed deeply, sadly, staring out at the water. For moments, he closed his eyes, trying to find a path forward.

"Do you believe they understand the damage this is causing?"

Malachi was sitting on the sofa in the cottage that he had created. Beside him, Nuance was nuzzling his hand. He'd thought from time to time about getting another dog, but deep down, he'd always known that she was irreplaceable. "I really don't like to attribute nefarious motives to people. Most of the time, the worst offenses are committed out of selfishness, carelessness, and you know."

"Ego?" Simon prodded, perching himself on the arm of a nearby chair. Even though he was a very old and wise soul, his friend/guide inhabited the body of a rather athletic spry young man. At times his energy seemed too large to be contained within the walls of Malachi's cozy cottage. Perhaps he might be more comfortable running a few laps around City Park.

"Yes, ego. I imagine they, the two, you know, felt quite puffed up in their first flush of success. It's addictive — power, particularly if one has little else to feel good about within themselves."

"Really? They are successful working women. Why so low a self-image?"

"It's all perception. This world is much too obsessed with comparing yourself with others to measure your real worth."

Simon smiled, "Thus, Annabelle Killian."

"Yes, I would imagine Annabelle looks to her cousin Irena and finds herself lacking. And perhaps wanting of the things she feels she should be entitled to."

"What a rabbit hole that is."

"Yes, of course, there is never peace seeking outward, not accepting and embracing one's path."

"How sad," Simon murmured once again on his feet. "And you are convinced they are using Annabelle to drain the spiritual energy of Irena Ellerman."

"It seems they have depleted and damaged Annabelle with their convoluted ceremonies, so they must use her, deceive her, gain more energy that she, of course, believes is for herself."

"So, she is complicit."

"To a degree, I suppose. She would like to believe that what they're doing, taking from Irena, has no real effect on her. But she is no fool. She is simply comfortable being deceived."

"So how to proceed, Malachi?"

Nuance yawned as he scratched her softly on the head. "Planting seeds, I'd imagine, planting seeds and seeing what takes root."

"What do you want?"

"To talk, that's all."

It wasn't an easy thing to place oneself inside another's dream. Then again, dreams weren't at all the manifestation of imagination that modern culture purported them to be. A creative act? Yes, of course, but the spirit, the soul, was a most creative entity creating all sorts of realities to experience and learn from that are never acknowledged by the physical self. The bottom line is that what we do with our physical lives is only a very small portion of where we live. Sometimes our astral traveling at night takes us to higher realms of reality, and sometimes our conscious choices trap us in lower/courser ones.

Such seemed to be the case of Annabelle Killian.

He looked around, scarcely recognizing where they were, but it seemed they'd never left her townhouse.

Malachi looked down. The carpet in her den was slushy, not firm. In fact, his feet had sunk down into it, the plush dark blue shag collapsing, enveloping him up to his ankles. She stood before him, Annabelle Killian but a different Annabelle. She'd mutated into a strange internal manifestation that projected itself externally in the dream state.

The woman before him was thin, not comfortably, fashionably thin, but starving, emaciated, and bony, not unlike photos he'd seen of concentration camp victims from World War II.

Her tattered, torn, and, yes, dirty nightshirt hung on her bony frame. Her long lanky, stringy dark hair surrounded the pale, thin face, its eyes wide and horribly afraid. It went beyond disturbing to see her like this, but he steeled himself. There were things to do here.

"I don't know you," she muttered in confusion. He could feel that much from her. She was perilously low on energy from the draining of Lydia Dressel and Jocelyn Accuro, so little energy left made her unable to think clearly.

"You don't need to be afraid, Annabelle," he said calmly, trying to be soothing.

"I don't want you here."

She stepped back away from him, and he heard the sloshy movement of her swampy carpet. He glanced around. There was fluttering, movement surrounding them. He exhaled, strong parasites, but just now, they weren't moving in, although in her present state, Annabelle was more than vulnerable to their attacks.

Again, he focused on the shell of the woman before him, eyes so wide and arms wrapped around her in the self-protection stance. "Annabelle, I want to help you."

He could feel fear emanating from her, but oddly he could feel something else as well. And then he took a sharp breath because he understood. It wasn't just fear. It was fear of being told the truth. She already knew. She already knew and feared it being confirmed.

Malachi understood at that moment that he had to be careful, had to approach the matter from a different direction.

"Annabelle, there is someone who needs your help."

Her expression changed, shifted a bit. Clearly, she was preparing herself for something different. "Who? What do you mean?"

"Your cousin Annabelle, your cousin Irena is in trouble."

She shook her head in negation. "That's not possible. Irena is fine."

"No, Annabelle, that's not true. She's being attacked. She is losing so much energy. Do you know who is attacking her, Annabelle?"

"No," she nearly whispered.

"Yes, of course, you do."

"I'm not hurting her."

"Of course, you are, you and Lydia and Jocelyn, all of you are hurting her. Why would you do that? Do you hate her so much?"

"It's not true. I don't hate her," she nearly whispered.

"Why would you let them attack her? You must hate her."

"No, it's not hurting her. They said that she could never tell the difference."

"They're lying to you. You are stealing her life energy. You are making her sick."

"No, no, they said."

"They're using you in their ceremonies so that you can steal energy from Irena. And then they drain you."

"No, no, that's not true."

"Yes, of course, it is. They know you. They have touched you. They have marked you in their ceremonies so that they can drain you."

"You're lying."

"You already feel the truth, Annabelle. You are starving because they are draining you. Don't lie to yourself. Don't let yourself be used to hurt someone else."

She fell to her knees in the slop that was her carpet, sobbing, just sobbing. Lightly, he put his hand on her head trying to seal the knowledge within her.

Beside him he saw a man standing, watching them both.

"You've been helping," Malachi murmured.

He spoke softly, "I've been trying to help. I'm near, but she can't see me yet. She is too blinded by what they've drawn her into."

Flashing through his mind Malachi saw glimpses of what could be — a new life for them, happiness, a path helping others. But she was allowing herself to be derailed.

"There is no guarantee," he said.

The younger man nodded. "I know. I can only try and help."

Malachi felt his heart clutch painfully. He was giving too much energy.

In the next moment, he felt himself rush back into his body. There wasn't much else to do now.

"So, you think I should cut off contact with her?"

"I do. It's best for now."

Irena looked a little uncomfortable at the prospect. But then again, Malachi had gleaned that she was a bit of a people pleaser. That was always a dangerous prospect, leaving one open to victimization. "I just hate to be rude."

"Sometimes it's necessary and warranted to protect oneself."

She nodded, then asked hesitantly, "So you think things will get better?"

"For you undoubtedly, Mrs. Ellerman. For others, well, that is really up to them."

She smiled tentatively, rising from the wicker chair on his porch to leave. Something about her reminded him of his late wife — a gentle spirit, but then again, someone who was beneath stronger than the most formidable adversary.

The Lost Soul

It's painful, perhaps too painful at times to be alive. In fact, occasionally, he felt drenched in it. Odd how negativity so completely drowns out gentler emotions — love, hope, even joy.

The fear feels like a raging animal filled with pain and madness, desperate to somehow alleviate it in any way possible.

He breathed in sharply, the emotion clinging acutely somewhere around his spine, specifically the lower back region. The solar plexus was usually where the more primal emotions were housed though he felt it everywhere.

Whoever said emotions weren't physical, well, was more than mistaken. The intensity of it made him ill.

He walked into the hallway of the apartment building. The ceiling was high, the floor a black and white terrazzo pattern — small blocks — rather nondescript, the doorways painted white, wooden.

Again, there was a wave of that intense emotion punching into his gut. How could anyone bear to live here?

"Numbness," his companion commented to him. He glanced next to him, a tall, stately, ebony-skinned young man dressed in his 19th-century English garb. Simon Tull was his sometime companion and his full-time spirit guide. He would see him, normally, when he traveled astrally — whether in dreams or as now on an excursion, an out-of-body excursion.

He was Malachi McKellan — primarily an esoteric author but, from time to time, a sort of paranormal investigator. He was in his mid-60s and felt, more often than not, that he was getting too old for this business. "One would have to be pretty numb to ignore this level of emotional disturbance."

"Most people achieve a cultivated numbness, dismissive of their feelings, or rather worse, attributing them to incorrect sources."

Another wave of fear hit him acutely right in the middle of his stomach. It was true that if he didn't understand this intense emotion did not belong to him, it would be extraordinarily disturbing to his peace of mind. He tried to clear his thoughts, separating himself from the unchecked negativity. But it was challenging. The place was thick with the cobwebs of unfiltered emotion. "It's difficult," he murmured.

"Yes, of course," Simon grimaced, continuing to walk beside him but letting Malachi take the lead. Simon never relinquished his role as a mentor or, perhaps more aptly put, guide. Though often disguised to help others, these exercises were still his learning ground. Simon's function was to nudge him, at times strenuously nudge him, in the right direction and also in the direction of Malachi's personal evolution.

He stopped near the end of the long hallway staring at a wooden door — one with a bold number eleven painted in black on its white surface. "Still alive?" he asked.

"Unknown," Simon answered.

And quite jarringly, even for those operating from the astral plane, the door flew open. Malachi stumbled backward a bit at the force of the action. In addition to the jolt of his sudden appearance, the man now before them was perfectly frightening. He was a young man early twenties, skinny, grizzled, unshaven, eyes wide with terror, face with a nearly yellow pallor. But it was the blood that was so evident, still running from the slashes he'd made on his wrists — some dried, caked on his clothing, but most still fresh, dripping out of the wounds.

"Are you the paramedics?" His voice rasped with fear. "I called days ago," and then he frantically clutched his wounds. "I can't get it to stop bleeding."

Malachi took a breath that felt like a knife of pain in his stomach. No, this one was definitely not alive, and that would make it much more complicated. "How long?" he murmured to Simon.

"About half a century," he answered softly, clearly not trying to further agitate the monstrously agitated young man.

Good Lord, imagine being trapped in your own psychodrama for half a century.

Two days earlier

"It's an older building right on St. Charles Avenue. I've no idea how long it's been there."

Malachi sipped his blueberry tea. It was purported to be good for his nerves, though at the moment, he couldn't really attest to that. He'd been stuck somewhere deeply in the abyss of writer's block when Adele Blanchard had dropped by unexpectedly to jar him further off course or perhaps just distract him a bit from his intended purpose.

"And your friend who looked at an apartment there, did she find something somewhere else?"

Adele seemed to perceptively bristle, straightening up in the rattan chair across from him on his screen porch. "Well, yes, she found a lovely place off of Henry Clay Avenue, but it's more than clear something is very wrong in that apartment building."

He nodded, noting her blueberry tea remained untouched on the glass coffee table in front of her. "You went there?"

"I was curious."

He put his mug down and leaned back in his chair, closing his eyes for a moment. "You were able to go inside?"

"Yes, I called, told them I wanted to look at the place."

"To rent for yourself?"

"Well, yes Malachi, otherwise —"

"Otherwise, they wouldn't have let you in." He opened his eyes, feeling a dull throbbing somewhere in the middle of his forehead.

"There is something very wrong there," she muttered.

"No doubt, clearly you lost quite a bit of energy."

"Do you think so?"

He shrugged. "Tell me what you felt."

"Let's see. The place was large, two-bedroom, with high ceilings but window units. Not so unusual for an older building."

He could concretely see the place in his mind as she described it. Quite unconsciously, she seemed somewhat adept at transferring visual images. "No, Adele, please. How did you feel there?"

"Oh yes, of course. Well, it did feel cold, oddly cold since it was such a warm day outside."

He could sense within the image the cold spots she'd felt. "What else?"

"I—" and she hesitated, shifting a bit in her seat, "I felt strange, as though it was difficult to breathe."

Clearly, she'd tapped into others' emotions there — powerful, tangible, negative emotions that translated physically. "You know you really shouldn't seek these places out."

"I thought you'd want to know Malachi. You know you're very gifted with these sorts of things. Maybe you could do something to help there."

"Not everything can be helped. Sometimes you have to simply let things be what they are," he commented, perhaps a tad too dryly, as he sipped his tea.

She did look a bit stunned, surprisingly, as though he'd reached out and slapped her across the face. "But you've been given such abilities, Malachi. I truly believe you should use them."

He leaned back in his chair with no comment. How could he possibly explain this to her? Somewhere along the way, his optimism and belief that he could fix and help every situation had dissipated. It had evolved into a sort of world-weary acceptance that every soul was involved in its self-created drama and, yes, at times, its self-created hell. And the truth was that there was very little on the whole that he could do to make much of a dent in the misery in this world.

"You must understand, Adele, that acceptance is often a vital part of life. People choose their paths for various reasons, not the least of which is learning. We should invariably spend less time judging what is good or bad but rather accept. We must allow others to go through life their own way instead of trying to force what we believe should happen upon them."

She sat up even more straightly, though he had not believed that was possible. Bristling further, yes, perhaps that was an apt description here. "Malachi, what are you here to learn yourself if you don't even try?"

He sipped his tea because it had cooled off enough to do so, and he sipped his tea because he did not know how to answer her. When should one accept, and when should one attempt to be of help? That was the question he had never quite found a proper answer to.

Over the next day and a half, Malachi sunk himself into his writing. Through his books, this was a tangible way he could help people, educate them about the spiritual nature of existence. But it was rough going. There was no easy flow to his thoughts nor any adhesiveness to his concentration. There was an impediment. And though he did not actively seek it out, he knew without question Simon would tell him that this was a message from the spiritual realm. It was telling him that he was ignoring a pressing matter.

So, he took a drive in his sky-blue sedan. It was late May, and the humidity of the summer was already beginning to devour the New Orleans landscape. At this point, all he could hope for was a strong thunderstorm to blot out some of the heat temporarily.

It bothered him, or rather Adele bothered him — her optimism, her naïveté, so to speak. Perhaps it had begun to overwhelm him, too much pain traveling to places and seeing things with a decidedly unique view that most people would never be conscious of.

He found it necessary to insulate himself from becoming too involved, not unlike a doctor who had to become detached from the suffering of their patients in order, well, not to absolutely drown in it. But how much was too much detachment? Was he slowly losing his humanity? And as Adele had suggested, what indeed was he here to learn?

As he drove past the palatial homes on St. Charles Avenue, he forced himself to put aside these cryptic self-reflecting considerations and obtain a clear mind. Such circular distractions could be of no help now.

He slowed his car as he approached the building. Adele had succinctly described its location before leaving. No matter what he'd said, she hadn't given up on him. He breathed deeply, focusing on receiving impressions like a blank slate.

But at least a block and a half before he came to the structure, it made its presence known with a stabbing pain directly in the middle of his forehead. The sensation was not so very unlike someone taking a rather sharp and pointy knitting needle and plunging it directly through the skin on that spot.

And as he actively drove by, it intensified quite decidedly. His breathing became labored, his skin clammy. He was more than sure anyone else experiencing these symptoms might surmise they were having a heart attack or stroke. But Malachi knew differently. He knew the symptoms of a spiritual attack. Nearly as though something had reached outward and struck at him directly.

"This isn't the first time I've been down that street, but I've never felt this magnitude of negative energy there before."

"Sometimes these things are cloaked, perhaps mostly confined to the structure's interior itself." Simon didn't always have all the answers, or if he did, he didn't always disclose them promptly. Malachi had noticed since their earliest association, which had actually been when he was a young teenager, that Simon Tull preferred for Malachi to puzzle out his own answers. A good tactic for a spirit guide, he supposed.

"Adele, Adele came into direct contact with the place. I suppose she might have functioned as a kind of conduit or even magnifier for me."

"Could be," Simon murmured, pacing in front of the fireplace of the mountainside cottage, actually the cottage that existed somewhere in a deeper level of Malachi's consciousness. It was where he and Simon would extensively hash out some of his dilemmas. And always here, it seemed to be perpetual November, which suited him quite well. "That is possible. Adele Blanchard is quite a sensitive, untapped as that may be."

Well, he did agree with Simon on that count. Although she liked to assume the façade of a bit of an eccentric, she did have an uncanny way of getting to the heart of the matter. "She was adamant about that place. That something was very problematic there."

Simon had stopped his pacing and was eyeing him curiously. "And you resisted her prodding?"

"Yes, I suppose I did. New Orleans is filled with all manner of psychic activities, divergent energies, and problem spots, if you will. How in the world does one know when to step in and when to leave well enough alone?"

Simon leaned back against the redwood mantle of the fireplace, seemingly lost in thought. "Well, I can tell you, my friend, it isn't an analytical decision. At times, you must act because there will be no peace within you if you do not."

When Malachi was nine, nearing ten as he recalled, though granted the recollection was not as crisp and jarring as it had been when he was younger, he and his family vacationed in a charming sort of beach house along the coast of Cape Hatteras in North Carolina. His father's work, consulting on engineering projects, actually had the small family rather mobile in those days. For him, it meant roots that were transferable, certainly not firmly grounded, and a younger sister as his one true friend.

But this summer had promised to relieve them all of some of the vexation and turmoil of their transient lifestyle. At least, that was the hope.

Cosmetically, and from old family photos he'd acquired upon his mother's death, he recalled the house as being quite lovely. Just a half dozen yards from the beach proper, white wood, spacious rooms, a long screen porch at the front, and a winding stairwell leading to the second-floor bedrooms.

Of course, even at nine, though he was not yet under the tutelage of his good and faithful mentor, one Simon Tull, Malachi had a radar for unusual phenomena. Even before he crossed the house's threshold, he knew something was wrong.

And on the third night of the occupation of their new residence, Malachi found out in particular what it was.

He kept his window open at night, allowing the sea breeze to fill his room. The white sheers fluttered as the illumination from the moon gave a tinge of variation to the darkened room.

Perhaps he'd been dreaming, but he awoke to the sound of rustling, movement.

It startled him, the figure standing at the window. He was only nine, but then reason stepped in. Perhaps it was his mother or sister. But no, his sister was not taller than him, and his mother, while a lovely woman, was well into her late thirties. This young lady in the long white nightgown was also not blond. Her hair was long and dark, dark like the shadows covering her.

His heart was pounding with fear as his analytical side concluded that this, indeed, was an intruder. "What do you want?" He called out in the steadiest voice he could pull out of his nine-year-old arsenal.

It was moments before he was acknowledged, but she did slowly turn toward him. Granted, the light was dim but even, so he marked the extreme pallor of her skin, not so different from the color of her nightgown nor the long rope hanging loosely around her neck. It was a noose.

But even with the ugly swollen welts around her throat, the most horrible thing was her eyes. They were so wide, so terror-filled, that he could feel her horror, her fear hitting him tangibly in the gut. He was a boy, not given to panic, but he was more than sure he screamed.

Of course, when all was said and done, his rescuers, his parents, attributed the episode to a bad dream. But he knew without question that it had not been.

"Suicides are a difficult lot," Simon had pronounced rather emphatically some years later. "Unfortunately, depending on the mitigating circumstances, they often bear the fate of a murderer."

Malachi did remember being somewhat befuddled at that proclamation. "That sounds a bit harsh."

"From a certain point of view, by killing our body, we are murdering ourselves. Do we have the right to destroy the physical vessel that houses the spirit any more than another has the right to destroy that vessel?"

"Yes, within suicide, we are only causing harm to ourselves. And I'd imagine someone who does it is just looking for an escape from pain," Malachi argued.

"Pain perhaps their spirit has chosen to learn from."

"All in all, it still seems a bit harsh."

"Well, judge it as you may, my friend. It does, however, hurl the one who does it into a rather protracted period of chaos, a fugue, if you will. That can last until they acknowledge and take responsibility for their actions. Only then can healing begin. That young woman you saw had been trapped in her own psychodrama for over a hundred years in your estimation of time."

"My estimation of time?"

"Another discussion Malachi, but the truth is that in attempting to escape pain, a suicide actually only inflicts more pain on themselves, self-created as it is."

Malachi took in the pitiful creature before him, feeling a curious case of déjà vu. He had all the hallmarks of a suicide trapped between realities that had been quite unconsciously haunting this old apartment building for some time. But nonetheless, something about this just didn't quite sit right with him.

He turned to Simon. "He can't be responsible for all the negative energy in this place."

Simon shrugged a bit expressionless. "Doubtful that he could be, more of a symptom, I'd imagine — though no doubt he has fed into the overall complexity of the situation."

He turned back to the fellow in question, who seemed to be eyeing both him and Simon with growing agitation. "Yes, of course, we called," he tried to say as pleasantly as he could manage. "But you really need to calm yourself."

His eyes widened in undeniable terror. "Look at my arms," he said, holding them out in front of him. "They won't stop bleeding. No matter what I do, they just won't stop."

"Yes, perhaps you just need a bit of a rest." He glanced inside the apartment, becoming aware of a rather pungent smell emanating from the interior. "What did you say your name is again, friend?" he asked.

The poor unfortunate glanced at Simon and then back to him suspiciously. "My name? Why do you need my name?"

"Don't push," Simon murmured.

He was right. Malachi could feel it acutely — the sheer horror and panic emanating from this lost soul — something that he found oddly disproportionate because clearly it wasn't all self-generated. Something or someone wanted to keep this one in a perpetual heightened state of anxiety. But why?

"Draining," Simon answered as though Malachi had spoken his thoughts aloud, but then again, it was true in this astral state that thoughts were more permeable, more accessible than normal. "Such a heightened level of upset makes energy draining much more easily accomplished."

Of course, that was true, and in the psychic or, dare he say, spiritual realm, energy was a commodity much sought after. It was more precious than gold to those who understood its real power — the life force: a force that, under the right conditions, could be stolen from unsuspecting victims.

"So, he is not the source," Malachi concluded. The young man glared at both of them wide-eyed and utterly panicked, responding as though what they were saying was complete gibberish. And he supposed, considering his realm of experience, that their conversation probably was.

"No, as I said, a symptom or, if you'd rather, a victim."

Malachi stepped back from this pitiful individual, trying to obtain enough distance to focus again on his surroundings. "There isn't a great deal that can be drained from an individual such as this caught between existences. Most of his energy is gone."

"Yes," Simon standing beside him again. "Unless he can be used as a tool, help create an atmosphere of anxiety in this place."

"To help facilitate the draining of the living," he finished Simon's thought. "But if he's been here over fifty years, what exactly is forcing him to stay."

"Something else," Simon murmured. "Something confusing him, suppressing him, using him for its own ends."

Hearing is an odd thing in the astral realm. Sometimes it functions like a thought in one's mind, and sometimes it is something quite physical akin to the sensation in the physical world. Malachi was more than certain that, in that moment, he heard a heavy footfall behind them.

Fifty-two years ago

"Your sister is in trouble."

He frowned. He was thirteen and heavily enmeshed in a new science fiction release. And at that point, he hadn't decided whether Simon Tull was real or just a figment of his overactive imagination.

But there he stood, big as life, in the middle of his bedroom, two o'clock in the morning while Malachi lay huddled in his bed holding a flashlight reading his new book. Perhaps he wasn't really reading. Perhaps Simon Tull was part of a dream within which Malachi was reading his book, though quite honestly, that seemed a little thin.

So, he put down the paperback and quite dryly commented, "Am I my sister's keeper?"

The tall, dark fellow glared at him a bit. "Are you daft, lad? To sit up on your high horse and quote the Bible at me as if you even understand what it means."

He shrunk a bit beneath the covers. The stern British tone disturbed him. "I don't know what you expect me to do."

"I expect you to help, young man. You're very gifted, and I expect you not to just sit on all that talent and piss it away."

He sat up in the bed, though, feeling a bit of outrage, making the hairs rise on the back of his neck. "I'm only thirteen. What do you expect, you ridiculous ghost?"

And then his face broke into a wide smile. "That's better. Now get out of bed, and let's see about your sister."

He was dressed in a t-shirt and pajama pants with no socks, of which he was acutely aware as his bare feet hit the cool wooden floor. "What's wrong with her anyway?" He didn't actually care for his sister just now at this stage of their lives. She was a pest, a pesky ten-year-old who always wanted to be in his business. She hadn't always been that way. His mother claimed it was a phase, a phase that, in his estimation, was going on entirely too long.

"Come with me," the tall, lanky, fellow commanded. He'd actually talked to him only maybe one or two times before, but he was always dressed the same, in that old-fashioned gray tweed suit. Awfully dressy for Malachi's boyhood bedroom, he thought.

Evangeline, or Evie as was her nickname, slept across the hall. The door was always opened because she was afraid of the dark. Simon Tull stopped short before they entered the room, putting his hand out in front of Malachi. "Now, lad, you might find this a bit upsetting at first. Keep your wits about you. That's the only way you'll be of any use to Evangeline."

He yawned, wishing now he could just return to his bed. "Fine," he muttered.

Simon Tull stepped back, allowing Malachi to enter first. But he didn't get far. In fact, he didn't get much more than two feet in the room.

Evangeline was there, seemingly asleep in her white metal daybed. The shocking thing, though, was that she wasn't alone. There was something with her, bent over her, something dark, darkish green, and moist. It seemed humanoid in some respects but with abnormally long, slimy wet arms and scaly skin. It moved or slithered a bit over her, then pulled its misshapen head up and turned to them. He didn't know if it had eyes. All he could see was a round hole where a mouth should be and long silvery teeth.

"It's a monster," he choked out.

"Calm down, Malachi. You won't be of any use so upset."

"What's it doing to her?"

"Draining energy, I'd imagine. Most children have a natural immunity to that sort of thing, but there is something about Evangeline that makes her vulnerable."

Its arms sort of unwound and slithered over his sister, almost as though it were making some sort of claim. "Why is it so hideous?"

"I think it's the only way your mind can translate it to your brain. It's a low one, a sub-parasite sort of creature. Looks like a monster to you because it lives on such a base plane of existence."

"What does it want?"

"What we all want deep down, to have a better life, to evolve, acknowledged or not. It feels that if it can absorb Evangeline's pure energy, it will gain strength, feel better."

"You said she's vulnerable."

"She's an empath. A pension for psychic abilities seems to run in your family. It must have approached her as something else — perhaps."

"An imaginary friend," Malachi completed the thought dubiously. She had rattled on and on about her imaginary friend. What was it? A koala or panda? Much to his chagrin, he couldn't recall.

"Yes, yes, and she's a lonely little girl, happy for company."

"But this thing?"

"Well, she doesn't see it as you do."

"So, monsters are real then?"

Simon Tull shrugged a bit. "There are all kinds of monsters in the world, Malachi. But what's clear is that we need to get rid of it before it makes her too weak and open to all sorts of other attacks."

"How do we do that?"

He smiled rather warmly, given their situation. "That's where you come in."

Malachi stood quietly within the halls of the Napoleon Apartment complex on St. Charles Avenue. It was difficult to think here, difficult to center himself as he was overcome with waves of disturbing concentrations of low-frequency emotions. Fear was paramount, anxiety of all sorts, panic, paranoia, and anger — fierce strands of anger always the stalwart companion of fear.

"Focus Malachi," Simon's voice from now or perhaps long ago. *"Fill yourself with calm, with peace, with love for your sister."*

He remembered it from the past. *"The feeders don't know what to do with those emotions. It confounds them. Then it terrifies them."*

He heard the movement behind him — the rustling. "Can you see it yet?" Malachi asked.

"Yes," Simon said quite solemnly. "This one has grown strong here — feeding for so long."

"What can I do against that?"

"It thrives on fear, young Mister McKellan, on all the base emotions. Even its appearance to you inspires this. So, you cannot give it what it wants, instead, give it what it does not want."

Slowly, he opened his eyes. It was in front of him now, moving, rasping as it moved. It had a huge misshapen head, long twisted arms, not unlike mangled and brittle tree branches. The eyes were red, a glowing indication of its energy frequency, and the skin the palest white. There were also clothes; tattered torn clothing suggesting that it had attempted to emulate human wardrobe. Is that what it aspired to, evolving to their level?

There were beings in the world who masqueraded as people, usually existing on the lowest rung of the evolutionary ladder. Base creatures still functioning largely as parasites, bent on exploiting what is worst in the human condition. Perhaps in all its energy accumulation, that was its ultimate goal.

"Possibly," Simon muttered, acknowledging Malachi's thoughts in his clipped British accent. "This whole place has functioned as a power charging station for this thing for decades."

It moved or slithered, perhaps was the proper description. "I don't think it likes me," he remarked. His skin felt hot. It wanted a way in, but his determination and focus were resisting it.

"We need to kick it out," Simon said rather placidly.

"How do we get rid of it?" He said a bit breathlessly. That's what it felt like being near the creature, that he was wholly out of breath.

"Be calm, Malachi. Do not be afraid of what you see. It's much more afraid of you than you are of it."

"How can that be?" asking a bit in disbelief.

"Because it feels your strength, the positive energy of your character, your energy, that is death to it."

"I'm not that positive."

"Do you want to hurt anyone?"

"No, of course not."

"Do you wish to help people?"

"Yes, that's what is right."

"Do you want to help your sister?"

He focused on her, seeing her toss and turn in her sleep and seeing that thing near her. "Yes, of course, I do."

"Then use all your concentration, Malachi, and surround her in white light, a protective cocoon that this thing cannot breach."

He stood there concentrating, reaching deeply into his imagination. There is a power in creativity. He remembered that from somewhere.

He could see the light all around Evie now, like a white glistening bubble surrounding her. He could feel peace, love, and a calmness that he could not remember truly ever tapping into before.

This will be your life — the voices whispered to him. You will help others and battle what seeks to attack.

It rasped and moved as though it had been hit by something. "That's good, Malachi. It drains through the eyes."

He zeroed in on the glowing red eyes, targeting and sending forth a pure belt of energy. It tumbled backward, slithering.

"It's strong, and it's been here too long. Remove its focus."

The frightened figure was crouching down a bit near his doorway, but whether or not he could actually see the thing was unknown. Malachi reached out for a name. "Henry," he called out. "It's time to move on."

He felt the initial rush of Henry's fear but tried to steady it with his energy. "Come, Henry, it's time to end the pain you've been living in and move on where there is help for you."

"No, no, I can't leave. It's not safe."

The thing rasped in anger, but Malachi ignored it. "Henry, you aren't safe here," he said as compassionately as he could muster. There had been many times during his life when he'd been called upon to help a spirit cross over who had lost their way. It was essential to be firm but comforting with them. They must feel your resolve but not be too afraid of you to trust. "Henry, you are being used, used to hurt others. Calm yourself and feel the truth in my words." He projected a powerful shower of energy in Henry's direction. He tried to help him sort past the fear that paralyzed him in order to hear the truth.

"I — I can't."

"Henry, they're waiting for you, the ones who love you." He could feel them just beyond the veil, just into the light. There was now the passageway to them opening in that dusky hallway where they all stood. They had tried for so long to reach out to him, but all their efforts had been muffled by the hunger of the thing still rasping behind them.

Henry rushed toward him. That was the key. He felt the tiny flower of hope in him. "My mother."

"Yes, Henry, she wants to see you again, but you must go to her."

He stopped in front of Malachi. Beside him, the thing writhed, reaching out its gnarled limbs toward Henry. Once it made contact, Henry flinched but didn't seem to see it.

"I can't," he muttered again, his energy being tapped by the beast. Malachi focused his energy toward it again, and it rasped painfully, breaking the contact. "You must. You cannot stay here any longer. It isn't safe."

"I don't know."

Malachi could feel his confusion. He'd been trapped here for so long, literally preyed on until he had so little will of his own left. "Henry, she needs you." He had to try to reach him. He looked up, confused. "Your mother needs you. Won't you go to her and help her?"

Henry looked around with an alertness in his eyes that Malachi hadn't seen before.

"Behind us," Simon said.

Malachi turned as he saw the tunnel of white beginning to open. He had to push his advantage. "Can't you hear her now, Henry?"

The tall gaunt man shuffled closer, and Malachi stepped back so he could see the tunnel. "That's where she is," he compelled. "Henry, you must go quickly." But he was wavering. Henry glanced around with confusion. The thing suddenly lurched toward him, but Simon jumped between them, intercepting the contact.

"Go, Henry. Run. She needs you."

The lost soul hesitated but only for a moment. Then, with an unexpected sprint that Malachi was amazed he even had within the emaciated body, he leaped toward the tunnel that seemed to immediately seal itself behind him.

"Good," Simon said, breathing deeply with marked fatigue. "That will make this much easier."

"What do I do?" He whispered, literally shaken to the core for the first time he could really remember in his thirteen years on this earth.

"Focus, envelop Evie in the white light, restore the natural barrier she should have to this kind of attack."

He tried. He focused with everything he had in him. His imagination was strong. It had always been that way, but it undeniably felt different this time. It pooled into a place of visualization where he could literally feel power in the form of energy flowing out of him. The thing moved, glided perhaps around the outer perimeter of the bubble he'd placed around his sister. It was trying to reestablish contact but seemingly unable to puncture the protection he'd placed around her. "Now strengthen it," Simon Tull's voice was calm but exacting.

He focused strength into the bubble, and almost instantly, the creature reacted — howling in some disturbing, indistinctive voice. Malachi could see liquid oozing out of it, ugly black seepage as though it had been wounded.

"What now?" He yelled to Simon because everything felt louder, as though a powerful storm was whipping around them all.

"Holdfast, boy, continue," he commanded.

He focused, focused acutely, until his head ached, his body stiffened with discomfort, and his vision began to spin. But he held on with the determination born of his innate stubbornness. He wasn't one to give way. It wasn't in his nature.

The thing continued to ooze in more places and twist in horrible unnatural contortions. "Good Malachi," he heard Simon's voice but couldn't see him. The storm was too loud. All he could see was the thing twisting and howling and Evie thrashing about in her frilly rose-colored nightgown as though she were trapped in some horrific nightmare.

He knew that he had to end this. His knees were trembling violently, and he wouldn't last much longer.

Malachi focused one last ditch effort and sent every ounce of strength he had left into the white bubble around his sister.

It landed powerfully, something like a mad surge of electricity. He saw the thing fling back violently against the far wall of the bedroom. It hit like an explosion, then broke into pieces with a fierce pop before it dispersed into a cloud of shimmery black dust that dissipated in the air.

He was breathing heavily, feeling as though he couldn't get any air. "Did we kill it?" He rasped to Simon, who was now standing beside him.

"Nothing ever really dies," he said a bit solemnly. "But it's changed into something else, perhaps a bit less virulent. I don't see it returning."

Malachi wanted to cheer, claim some sort of victory, but instead, the shakiness overtook him as he sunk to his knees. "What's wrong with me?" he murmured, feeling the peculiar pressure of Simon's hand on his shoulder, given that he believed he was a ghost.

"You're dangerously low on energy now, Malachi. You must rest. You saved your sister, my boy, be happy."

It moved and rasped in confusion in the hallway. "Henry was its conduit, its bridge to draining the living here. Now it's disconnected from its energy source."

Malachi nodded. He could feel that. Simon's words were accurate. But he could also feel that the thing was very old, and it would be difficult to dislodge it from its current residence. "If we leave it here, will it simply diminish over time?" Malachi asked.

"Hard to say," Simon said grimly. "I don't think we're equipped to drive it off. It's too entrenched."

Malachi felt a heaviness inside his heart. It bothered him to acquiesce to the reality that some things were beyond him. Some things he couldn't resolve neatly. "I suppose we could do damage control. Keep an eye from time to time to ensure it's not exploiting some other lost soul as it did to Henry."

"Yes, I suppose," Simon said dryly. "Better if the place could be leveled in the earth and scorched."

Malachi laughed a bit, "Yes, in a perfect world, my friend, in a perfect world."

Obsession

"If I were man, this wouldn't be such an issue."

Adele Blanchard struggled to hold onto her pleasant demeanor in the presence of the young woman in front of her. She was reading her tarot cards. She didn't do palms. That was Annette's job, but occasionally Adele did still read Tarot cards in addition to attending to the day-to-day operations of her esoteric bookstore, The Blue Pelican. It was as much for herself as anything. She enjoyed reading the Tarot for customers, playing off the vibes she received from them, digging deep into her intuitive gifts while using the symbolism of the cards as a bouncing-off point. Usually, she gained as much from the endeavor as those she read for, usually. But this one, Suzanne Evons, she couldn't seem to get her to focus on what Adele was saying. Rather, she was purely focused on the one that got away.

"Oh, I don't know about that, Suzanne," she murmured as jovially as she could manage. "Unrequited love, unfortunately, when taken to extremes, can turn into harassment — male or female in question."

She bristled noticeably. In fact, she found that young Suzanne Evons tended to bristle whenever she didn't readily agree with her. "Are you implying that I'm harassing Joe?"

She delivered in a stringent tone bordering on indignant.

Adele steeled herself inwardly, continuing to shuffle the oversized deck of Rider Waite cards. It was difficult keeping calm. Something about this woman had raised her hackles from the moment they met. This would be the second elaborating spread she was doing for Suzanne as the original and the one following didn't seem to penetrate her rather tunnel vision perception.

"No, I didn't say that. Joe, of course, would have to be the one to determine if he was feeling harassed or not." And then she smiled to temper the sharp edges of her observation.

Suzanne's face seemed to only harden at Adele's remark. Her sharp cheekbones seemed to set as though carved in stone, and her well-sculpted eyebrows froze over her long almond-shaped eyes in an expression of determination. She was an attractive young woman, an ER nurse, no doubt a catch. So why was she so resolutely focused on a man who clearly wasn't interested anymore?

"I'm sure you're wrong, Ms. Blanchard. Once Joe remembers how good we were together, he'll wake up. I'm sure he'll value and appreciate the fact that I didn't give up on us," she stated rather flatly.

And invoking what Adele considered her minuscule repertoire of psychic gifts, she definitely sensed a wall here. There was a block in Suzanne's thinking where reason, reality, and good common sense just did not seem to penetrate.

I honestly can't account for it, Malachi. Love, lust, obsession — whatever you might want to label it, that sort of nonsensical determination will lead to trouble, maybe even of the criminal sort.

She was sitting out on Malachi McKellan's screen porch with his lovely view of the Bayou St. John and sipping tea — something fruity, blueberry or raspberry, or something of the sort. He had said distinctly that she needed calming before they sat down to talk. He was very sensitive to those sorts of things. And it was true. She was extremely agitated. The problem was that this whole matter incensed her to no end. The why exactly she couldn't say, except that she felt an instinctive dislike of Suzanne Evons.

"And how did the appointment end?"

"Well, I spread the cards again, which advised for the third time the same thing. Move on. Let the fellow do the same. But to no avail. It was absolutely as if I was talking to a brick wall, then she left."

He shrugged, "Young love."

"More like obsession." He leaned back on the rattan sofa, smiling a bit, she thought. She amused him, though exactly why her frustration amused him was beyond her. "Are you taking this seriously, Malachi?"

"I always take you seriously, Adele. You have a powerful though admittedly, raw psychic radar. I find you quite infallible."

"So, what do we do?"

"Do? Well, nothing at the moment, I'm afraid. Ms. Evons' obsession, I'm afraid, is just that, her obsession."

"But she could very well ruin her life over it."

"Yes, she might. But it is her life to ruin."

"Energy vampire?"

"Yes, no question, a young one, unconscious of it, but undeniably caught up in the thrall."

Nuance sat perched on one end of the tan suede sofa in Malachi's mountainside cabin. It was where he and Simon Tull, his spirit guide, met to hash things out, so to speak."

"You don't seem inclined to do much here, Malachi."

He scratched Nuance's head. She was nuzzled up against his leg. "Do you know how high a percentage of the population are energy vampires, Simon?"

"Of course, it's a significant rung in the ladder of spiritual evolution."

"Yes, something no doubt both you and I experienced in some former life," he said a bit distastefully.

"No doubt more than once, my friend. It's a hard lesson to fully absorb. That you have power, and yet you must learn not to use it."

"That's one way to look at it," Malachi scoffed.

With a big smile, Simon tapped him on the shoulder. "And what's another way, my old friend?"

"Learning not to be a parasite, sucking the energy out of your fellow human beings, and in effect compromising them and yourself."

"Not everyone is vulnerable."

"Yes, I know. Just the ones a little lost, searching for their next path." Softly, he commented, "Yes, those in between, but they manage to sniff them out readily enough, exploit them, steal their energy."

Simon frowned, "They're not evil, you know. Mostly it's unconscious."

Malachi shrugged, "One can feel what's positive or negative even if they choose to ignore it."

"It's all learning, my friend, no judgment, just learning."

"Yes, as you say," Malachi said a bit dubiously.

"So, are you going to help?"

"Help who, poor hapless Joe?"

"No, help Suzanne Evons."

"Suzanne — the vampire?" Malachi said with a bit of surprise.

"Yes, before she destroys herself."

In the evening, Malachi took a long walk down to the metal footbridge that connected Moss Street to its other half, crossing the tranquil waters of Bayou St. John. It bothered him, the feeling that whatever he did, however, he chose to help, was seemingly inconsequential in the vast scheme of things.

His hands rested on the metal railing of the footbridge as he stared out onto the darkening waters before him.

"It sounds like a dark night of the soul, Malachi."

He didn't look up. He knew the voice. He would have known her voice anywhere. She didn't come around often, not often in his dreams or even in his imagination. He believed that if she did that, he might just cease living altogether and drown himself in those few precious moments when he was in her presence again.

"It must be pretty bad if you're making an appearance."

"Maybe you just need a jolt or a kick." Her graceful hand softly took hold of the metal rail beside his.

"I've missed you, Josie."

She laughed softly, "You keep busy enough trying to save the world, except when you won't."

He glanced up. She looked young, maybe into her thirties, not as she looked when he'd lost her nearly fifteen years before. Then she'd been ill. It had been a long-protracted illness before she finally let go, leaving him to find his way alone in the world.

He breathed in her presence. It was intoxicating. Yes, he remembered love, and he remembered loss as well. "Whatever I do doesn't seem to make a difference."

She smiled. "It makes a difference to those you help, even if you can't help them all. It makes a difference to them."

"I'm tired, Josie."

Again, that incandescent smile, "I know my love. But there are still miles to go, so many miles."

He decided to focus on Adele. He sat in his den, candles lit, and put himself into a meditative state. He could see Adele clearly in his mind's eye. Using her as a starting point, he allowed himself to be drawn with her into her meeting Wednesday at The Blue Pelican with Suzanne Evons. It took place in a room at the back of the store, a small room that Adele had furnished almost as an old-fashioned Victorian sitting room with a splash of New Age. Intricate esoteric tapestries hung on the wall, and several vintage-looking lamps that reminded him a bit of steampunk with ornate shades sat on small antique-looking tables. There was a short pink velvet, serpentine loveseat, and two rosewood parlor chairs covered in a deep burgundy striped satin facing the intricately carved mahogany card table. Adele had undeniably spent some time thoughtfully decorating the room, reaching for just the right atmosphere to conjure up the image of a Victorian séance.

But as he looked closely at Adele's companion, he could see that all the ambiance seemed lost on her. She was, and he was trying to summon the proper word —

"Pragmatic," Simon completed for him.

His companion was now standing just to the side of Adele's chair. The women were silent, motionless, almost frozen in a tableau as he analyzed the situation. "I was wondering if you would make an appearance."

"As did I, I thought to leave you to your own devices, but my curiosity won out."

"She seems a bit cold."

"Oh, I don't know about that," he said, eyeing the tall brunette with expertly styled bangs fluttering across her forehead. "Certainly not terribly romantic, but undeniably a girl who knows what she wants."

"And that's Joe."

He shrugged, "She thinks so in any case."

"But not romantic?"

"I believe the word of the day is pragmatic. She feels she needs Joe for her life to progress as she envisions."

"And that's not cold."

"Perhaps, but I don't know. Some of us like our romance wrapped up in flowers, music, and pretty poems. And others in necessity, as things you must have like food, medicine, a car."

Malachi sighed, "And that's love?"

"Oh, I didn't say anything about love."

"You lost me."

"All right, think about your wife, Josie."

He frowned, "I'm not interested in discussing my wife, Simon."

He held up his hands as if felling off an attack. "Yes, yes, old boy, nothing personal, but if you knew you were causing her upset, distress, would you continue?"

"Of course not. If she wanted me to or had wanted me to, I would have left her alone instead of trying to force what I wanted on her."

"Yes, exactly, the difference, but Lady Suzanne here feels justified in pressing her expectations, her needs, her desires with no contemplation on how it might cause distress to poor Joe. In a nutshell, she wants what she wants, and everyone else be damned."

"Not love."

"No, not love, need perhaps, inexplicable determined need."

Malachi murmured in fatigue. "Of course, but she calls it love."

"Indeed, justification is a handy tool."

"So, how to reach her?"

"Yes, that is the question. Perhaps make the cost too high."

"Too high?"

"Yes, let's start with Joe."

Joseph Orusco worked for an insurance company — car insurance, health insurance, life insurance, whatever your pleasure might be. He was a young businessman just into his thirties who liked to spend his weekends playing tennis or racquetball.

"Doesn't seem like a complicated fellow," Simon commented dryly.

Malachi and Simon had traveled deep into the next evening and now stood in Joe Orusco's bedroom, quietly pondering their next move.

"I see your thread. Why such a commotion from Suzanne? Yes, okay, of course, the draining. Addiction to the energy she's gaining from him." Malachi glanced across the bedroom to the set of sliding glass doors leading out onto the patio. Quite clearly, through the open blinds, they could see a familiar figure in a long black nightgown pacing the pavement. She just kept walking back and forth in front of the window, not looking up at them once.

"Relentless might be the word," Simon muttered.

"I imagine if we weren't here, her astral self would be inside draining Joe relentlessly, as you say."

"Yes," Simon murmured. "She is still draining through their bonds, but not as much as if she were closer and not nearly as much as if they were in actual contact."

"Even more, of course, if it were intimate contact."

"Quite so."

Malachi stared at the sleeping figure of Joe Orusco, tossing around fitfully in the bed. With a bit more concentration, Malachi could actually see a faint flow of energy, looking a bit like a translucent beam of light-colored blue-green, moving from Joe's heart area toward the outside wall where Suzanne's astral self was holding its vigil. "The addiction goes both ways," Simon murmured.

"Yes, I suppose he has a taste for it, addiction to the draining, even if he is trying to break away."

"I wonder just how hard he is trying."

Malachi stepped back from the king-sized bed. "Let's find out, shall we."

He put his hands together and sank himself into a focused concentration reaching out to the deeper, spiritual self of the man in the bed. Within moments, the astral self of Joe, still wearing the same sweat-soaked New Orleans Saints t-shirt, sat up and stood, entirely separating from his physical self that remained in the bed.

His short-cropped, brown hair seemed damp, and his eyes were somewhat unfocused when he finally acknowledged Malachi. "What are you doing here?"

Malachi tried to appear pleasing. "Mr. Orusco, my colleague and I have come to talk to you and hopefully be of aid."

He looked around with confusion, then to Simon, who he eyed up and down a little warily in his vintage tweed suit. "Am I dreaming?"

Malachi responded a bit energetically as he suddenly felt anxious to be done with this business. "In a manner of speaking, Mr. Orusco, this conversation you will remember as a dream, but that does not make it in the least bit not real. In fact, perhaps very essential to your well-being, do you see right now who is pacing across your patio, Mr. Orusco?"

In the instant of a thought, the three of them were back in his den, standing in front of the sliding glass doors. Joe frowned, looking over Malachi's shoulder at the woman now staring longingly through the glass. "Son of a bitch, that's Suzy out there. I told her this was over."

"Apparently, she didn't get the memo," Simon muttered under his breath.

"Why don't we sit down, Mr. Orusco, and have a chat."

"Yeah, well, okay, is she just going to stay out there all night?"

"Hard to say," Malachi responded.

Joe Orusco had a small kitchen table in his condo, espresso colored, lighted by a low-hanging brass chandelier situated over the table. The three of them settled in for a discussion as Malachi debated the correct approach to the problem at hand.

"Mr. Orusco," he began.

"Everyone calls me Joe," he commented a bit obtusely, still appearing more than a bit disoriented.

"Joseph," he began again. The old adage that everyone understands from their own level of perception kept ringing in Malachi's ears. Joe, even for a white-collar working fellow, he could feel, was rough around the edges. He operated from a place of pragmatism, possibly more concerned with the comforts of the material world. This, more than anything, could have been his initial attraction to Suzanne Evons. "Tell me, are you in love with Suzanne?"

The tall, well-muscled fellow focused on him a little blankly. Perhaps it was the effects of being in an astral state, or perhaps it was his fallback demeanor, at the moment, hard to say. He shrugged. "Honestly, Suzanne is a great girl. We had a great run, but I'm looking to see what else is out there."

He heard Simon beside him sigh deeply. And he wondered, for not the first time this evening, why he was even trying. "So, I take it you have fully severed the relationship."

Joe leaned back in the chair, absently strumming his fingers on the espresso-colored tabletop. "For the most part."

Malachi caught the explicit frown that placed itself on Simon's face. "What the devil does that mean for the most part?" His speech had slurred a bit back into his cockney English accent, which tended to happen when Simon got irate.

"I mean, well, we've been together a few times since we broke up."

Malachi pressed for clarification. "By together, you mean intimate?"

"Well, you know, yeah, sure, I guess so."

Simon shook his head, saying nothing. So, it was clear Joe's firm feet were undeniably feet of clay, which would mean mixed messages.

"Yes, well, Joseph, I'm going to tell you some things that you may or may not remember tomorrow morning. But you should remember your emotional reaction, if nothing else. Suzanne is what we call an energy vampire. She has been draining your spiritual energy. That is why you have been feeling tired, unfocused, excessively emotional, having problems concentrating, problems with sleep, perhaps inexplicable pains in your body, in your chest, and in generally poor health."

Joe was looking a bit befuddled, but again perhaps a fallback expression. "I thought I'd just been pushing too hard at work."

"The low energy will make it difficult to function in all areas of your life."

"Why would she do that to me?"

"It's not conscious on her part, just something that she does. But it's up to you to cut her off."

Joe seemed confused again, but Malachi could understand that this was a lot to take in. "Suzy, well, is persistent. She was very unhappy when I asked her to move out, angry and really upset. And I didn't want to seem like a total jerk."

"You were living together? That makes the draining much worse, much more chronic." Then Simon directly lit into Joe with evident distaste. "You'll have to be a jerk. It's best for you and actually a kindness to her. So, she'll hopefully fill her life with other pursuits."

"Yes, in a nutshell, Joseph, no contact, particularly intimate contact," Malachi continued to pound the point. "The closer you are to her, the stronger the energy bonds she has with you. It is best to sever all contact, even if that means a restraining order."

"How could I do that?"

"You must. You must not equivocate. You must make it clear she is out of your life for good. No backtracking, Joseph, no communication, no phone calls, no emails, no texts, no contact at all. Do you understand?"

"Yeah, I think so."

"Joseph, look at me," Malachi said strongly.

It startled him. That was good. He wanted to scare him, so the impression was deeply embedded. "This is a dangerous matter. It will end badly if you do not heed me. Follow my instructions to the letter. No contact Joseph, even if you have to move, even if you change your phone number. No contact, Joseph."

Joe Orusco nodded slowly, but Malachi wasn't satisfied. He needed to drill it in so that the impression wasn't pushed aside in the morning light. "Repeat what I said."

"No contact."

"With whom?"

"No contact with Suzanne."

"Again."

"No contact with Suzanne." That night Joseph Orusco repeated the mantra one hundred times. Malachi suspected that Simon thought he was being excessive, but he said nothing.

As far as Malachi was concerned, Suzanne wouldn't see reason, so Joe was the only hope. When Malachi finally returned to his body, he felt as though he'd expended all of his energy trying to leave Joe with enough concern in his heart that he might actually stay away from Suzanne. There was no guarantee, but he'd tried and tried his best. So, he slept, a heavy sleep devoid of any travels.

"I haven't seen Suzanne Evons again. I thought about calling her to see how she is."

"Best to let it go, Adele." They were taking a late afternoon walk along the perimeter of Bayou St. John. She'd shown up at the house earlier, and he'd felt a remarkable draw to be outside, no doubt in need of the healing energy that nature could afford him.

"Do you think it will work out for her, Malachi?"

"Hard to say, my friend. We all have free will and ultimately are responsible for our destiny."

"Yes, but we can't anticipate everything that happens to us."

"No, of course not, but how we navigate the waves that crash on our shore. Well, that is always our choice."

Nuance

He walked around on his bare feet. That she remembered of him as a boy. The little girl wore socks or furry slippers, but the boy, Malachi, always had bare feet. Bare feet that she licked often — to clean because he needed cleaning.

"Nuance" was what they called her. She would quickly barrel up and down the wooden steps in the wood frame house when she heard her name called.

Then they stopped calling, and everything changed.

He scratched her head. She liked being scratched. She had a lot of fur, so it always felt good being scratched.

"Nuance has been traveling." The tall, dark-skinned man, he was Simon. She knew some language, enough that seemed important to her.

"Has she?" Malachi laughed, continuing to scratch her head softly. That was Malachi, her Malachi. She remembered him from all his life, as a boy, as a man, and now an older man. And not long ago, she visited them all.

Simon Tull was staring at her, seeing things. He'd been with her too. She followed him after the first passing.

"It's all right, Nuance," he'd said. She sniffed at the quiet body lying in a box on the kitchen table. "Time to go." It felt odd, so much lighter. All the aches and pains of age and illness gone, and she wanted to run, just run.

There were others there too. There was the tall black lab — Goliath, who left before she and another dog, a small white poodle. "That's Fancy. She'll be Evie's dog in a few years."

She would still hear the voices, Malachi upset and even crying openly, but it felt distant as another door opened.

"Where do you think she's been?" Malachi asked. He stopped scratching her, and she nuzzled closer to him to remind him to start again.

"Well, she's always close to you. She's very attached. But she is a reality hopper."

He laughed deeply. She was next to him, so she felt the warm energy of his laugh reverberate. She glanced around the room. He created it, but there were so many other things here that he didn't see. On the floor were five different versions of her — two young puppies tussling and a much older version of her lying quietly by the fireplace.

And the white dog, it just sort of watched, glowed, and soaked everything in.

Simon was watching her, then them. He could see them but not Malachi. The first time she saw the white dog, she was afraid.

"It's all right, Nuance. She's part of you, a higher part."

At times, she seemed like just another dog, circling her, pushing her with her nose. Then she fell asleep and dreamed she was the white dog.

She was lying in the kitchen at the McKellan house, but her paws lay on the linoleum floor. All around her were great colors shooting out from everywhere, and she heard a great hum in her ears. It was as though she was flying while being still, and she was happy.

Then she woke up and saw the white dog next to her.

At night, she still slept at one end of Malachi's bed curled up. And then they'd go for long walks outside, and she'd run. They're still together, but sometimes he doesn't know it, though most of the time he does. She nuzzles him, and he scratches her ear.

The Hotel

At first glance, there seems to be an infinite number of them tucked away in New Orleans, small hotels expanded from a former residential townhouse complex or renovated historic public building in the city, small hotels which on average only house ten to fifty rooms.

She stopped typing. Hook, you need to hook the reader right at the offset. This was a feature story, not a news story, after all.

Such is the case with the Maison du Bienville located deep within the city's French Quarter. A former palatial residence originally built in the 1730s and renovated in the 1790s, the Bienville was originally a porte-cochere townhouse converted in the 1950s to function as a thirteen-room hotel. Its elegant suites open directly onto Royal Street or face inwardly toward the hotel's lush garden courtyard.

She stopped pounding on the small portable typewriter she'd brought from home. Really, she should just write this out in long-hand until she got a handle on what she wanted to say, less waste of paper that way. Unfortunately, that was the problem. What exactly did she want to say? At present, it just sounded like a brochure for the Maison du Bienville. The story needed an angle, a different, fresh, sharp angle, if she was going to break into writing features at the Times-Picayune. Even though she'd only been working there as a junior news reporter for six months, already she was fighting a restlessness, the gnawing awareness that she should be doing something else.

"What's the problem?" her roommate and long-time friend Lucy Serio pushed the question. "You have your foot in the door. You're building a resume." The two girls shared a two-bedroom apartment in Metairie.

It was impossible to articulate that something relentless was pulling at her from the inside. So, this weekend, she'd given her brainchild legs and booked a room for a few nights in one of New Orleans' hidden treasures. Close exposure hopefully would enable her to cook up something exciting. Undeniably, the Maison du Bienville was unique. Its mysterious dusky red stucco exterior drew her acutely every time she drove by. Perhaps its paranormal reputation had pricked her interest, difficult to say. But now she was here and coming up with little to speak of.

She glanced despondently up at her reflection in the large mirror atop the ornate cherry wood dresser. The young woman staring back at her looked a bit pale and on the thin, willowy side, as her mother described it. There was medium-length, straight brown hair, bangs, high cheekbones, and rather large hazel eyes. And rounding it all out was a small but full mouth and an overall expression that denoted a bit of distance. Some might and had described it as cold, but she had always known it was nature's clever way of covering shyness — a shy woman who chose a profession where she had to interact with people fairly regularly.

"Do you really want to spend time in those creepy old hotels alone?" Lucy, again, Lucy was an elementary school teacher. She had quipped back rather quickly that she found Lucy's profession somewhat scarier.

"Yes," was, however, the answer that she expressed silently. She liked spending time in these creepy old places and spending time alone. Having a roommate was prudent just now, but the idea of having a place all to herself, now that was appealing. The truth was that people, most people, sort of tired her out.

"You know, some of those old places in the French Quarter are supposed to be haunted." Lucy, while being a very nice person, could be considered on the pushy side of the spectrum.

"I don't believe in ghosts," was her reply.

She wasn't sure if that was exactly true. What was true was that she would love to see a ghost. She'd love to write about seeing a ghost. Perhaps that was why she'd picked the Maison du Bienville. It had all those spooky stories attached to it, though perhaps just concocted to draw interest.

In any case, today was Friday. Lucy had dropped her off, and she'd checked in at exactly 3:00 PM. Checkout was Sunday at noon. Surely that must be enough time for concentrated exposure and, hopefully, insight or at least inspiration. Taking pictures, soaking up the atmosphere, doing some research, perhaps interviewing the staff and clients — either this would fly or crash dismally, and then she would just let the whole idea go.

The room itself was spacious. One of its interior walls was made of brick, while its French doors led out to the courtyard, which had a lovely picturesque swimming pool to one side.

She walked outside, breathing in the warm, sunny air. At the center of the courtyard was a brick-laid fountain where artistically fashioned, cast iron blue herons spewed a continual stream of water from their beaks. And on either side were half a dozen patio tables and black wrought iron metal chairs.

The hotel itself seemed oddly inactive, though, of course, it was still early in the afternoon. All the tables in the courtyard were presently unoccupied except just one. A few tables down, a man was sitting alone. As it was only the two of them, she couldn't help but stare. At first glance, he seemed on the youngish side. He wore glasses and was reading a book. She looked away, but then her eyes casually drifted back to him. He didn't appear to have noticed her. No, not very old, around her age or slightly older. She had just made twenty-five last month.

She clenched the small notebook in her hand. The idea had been to sit and write impressions, but at that moment, something else surfaced — perhaps a more personal angle. Taking a deep, steadying breath, she put on her reporter demeanor— affable but business-like.

Striding forward, she did not allow herself to overthink as she stopped abruptly in front of the man in question.

Taking only a brief pause, "I'm so sorry to disturb you, but I am a reporter from the Times-Picayune writing an article on the Maison du Bienville, and I was wondering if I could possibly interview you."

He didn't seem at all surprised. In fact, there didn't seem to be any reaction at all. Eying her calmly, he removed his dark-framed glasses, laying them down on the wrought iron table. Then rather methodically, he closed his book, not taking his eyes off her. His eyes, she could see clearly now, were a shade of deep blue.

In only seconds, a wave of second-guessing passed chillingly over her. This could be construed as an intrusion. "I, of course, would understand if you'd rather not," she muttered quickly.

And then he spoke. He had a voice that was deep and decidedly cultured. "Would you care to sit?"

She smiled a bit gratefully, awkwardly taking the seat across from him. "Thanks, I hope I haven't bothered you. I just thought it would be interesting to talk to some of the hotel's patrons about their impressions, a more personal view."

Then he smiled a nice smile. He had dark hair, dark brown, and was wearing a sports coat with matching tan pants and a dark blue shirt. Not too casual, but not a high-end business suit either, middle of the road, she'd have to say. She'd gotten into the habit with her job of making these quick, detailed evaluations. She was wearing her usual reporter garb, a paisley skirt with a black sweater and black boots aiming not to be too casual nor too dressy.

"That sounds like a good plan," he commented smoothly, somehow effortlessly dispelling her anxiety.

She laughed, "Well, we'll see. I mean to say that so far, my ideas of how to approach this haven't worked out as well as I'd hoped."

He tapped his book with his fingertips. "I can understand that. I'm also a writer, more of historical pieces, so I am familiar with trying different avenues."

"Oh, is that why you're here, working on something?"

"Yes, in a way, I suppose, Miss?"

"Oh, I'm so sorry, Josie Fleming."

"Ah," he held out his hand, and she grasped it briefly to shake. But long enough to feel it, just the brief contact that felt, for lack of a better word, charged. "My name is Malachi McKellan."

She softly pulled her hand away, landing somewhere between unsettled and surprised. "That's unusual, Malachi. Isn't it biblical?" she murmured.

"A prophet, I think. My parents were drawn to the unusual."

"I was named after Josephine March, Little Women, kind of destined to become a writer, I suppose."

"And how's that going?" he asked.

"Mostly well, though news reporting can be a bit dry. That was why I'm trying to break into features."

"Thus, the hotel."

She laughed, a bit of a nervous habit, "Yes, well, still looking for a different angle. Do you like it here, I mean the Bienville?"

It seemed like an ordinary question, benign enough, but a strange expression crossed his face. And she felt, for almost an inexplicable reason, that he didn't actually like the hotel at all. "It certainly is historical and quite an impressive place."

The pen that she was holding, she suddenly clicked impulsively. "That feels a little evasive, Mr. McKellan." Immediately, she wished she could jump back in time and put the words back into her mouth. Why did she say that?

But he seemed unflustered, laughing shortly at the comment, "I don't mean to be Miss Fleming. But I've always found most places to be complicated, often more than meets the eye."

"Oh, then you might be referring to the Bienville's reputation for being haunted."

At that, he did look at her a little oddly. "Is this something you want to talk about, Miss Fleming, whether or not the Maison du Bienville is haunted?"

The intensity she felt behind his question caught her rather off guard, so she considered it seriously. Was this something she wanted to talk about? She sincerely doubted that it was something she could write about in more than a peripheral way for the piece she was doing. But something, something about his casual but pointed question made her plunge forward. "Yes, actually, I would very much like to know what you think."

He nodded in acknowledgment, lightly strumming the surface of his book she noted for the first time was a volume called *The Secret Doctrine* by Helena Blavatsky—quite a hefty book from what she could see. "Then I suppose the short answer is yes. I believe this place is unquestionably haunted."

It was more than strange how disconnected the moment felt. In some respects, it seemed as though perhaps she'd imagined what she'd heard Malachi McKellan say to her. Within the confines of the world she knew, the world she'd grown up in, and the one she functioned within daily, it didn't feel like a particularly sane thing to express.

"So really, I mean, you really think this place is haunted?" she sort of stumbled through the words.

His eyes seemed to sparkle a bit, curiously as though her reaction amused him. "That surprises you, Miss Fleming?"

"I—I don't know. I suppose it surprises me that someone would just say it outright as though it's a fact. Things like hauntings, ghosts, are always hinted at, maybe laughed at a bit, but most people don't, well, don't—"

"I see. Take it seriously. It falls into the realm of superstition, fanciful territory if you will."

"Yes, I suppose, but you, you don't see it that way. Have you had experiences before with—" She sort of drifted off, feeling uncomfortable even voicing what she needed to voice.

"Ghosts, spirits, the paranormal?"

"Yes, I suppose that's what we're talking about."

"What if I told you that I had?" And then, oddly, he leaned in a bit. "What if I told you that the Maison du Bienville is a very complicated place, and that was why I was here?" There was something unexpected in his eyes, something nearly challenging. "Would you believe that I had lost my senses, Miss Fleming?"

She smiled a little awkwardly. "Not necessary. I suppose I'd want to ask why. Why it's so complicated, as you say."

Again, he lightly tapped the book in front of him as though considering. "Do you know much about this area? I mean, its history?"

"You mean the land itself? No, just in a very general sense."

"Well, what most people don't understand is that land, structures, and houses, for a variety of reasons, are not neutral in their energy. They often carry their own signature energy predisposed to attract events and entities of the same frequency."

"Frequency? I'm not sure I follow."

"To be plain, long before any structures existed here, this particular plot of land became tainted or soured, if you will. As a result, both indigenous people and early settlers most likely experienced increasingly calamitous events encouraged by the area's natural negativity."

"Negativity? So, you're saying this area where the Bienville is built has a natural negativity."

"Yes, that's exactly what I'm saying. The truth is that through its history, it has attracted and invited tragedy, and as a consequence, there are at present lost spirits trapped on the premises and others, less benign, as well."

"So, you do seriously believe it is haunted?"

"Yes, I do."

"And this negative nature that you say it has, can't anything be done to correct it?"

He sighed a bit wearily. She thought, "That's unclear. Sometimes through prolonged spiritual cleansings, scorching of the earth, exorcisms in the old days, and perhaps various ceremonies, the signature energy could be influenced, but more often than not, it is simply too embedded."

"Embedded," she repeated absently, as her mind was whirling. "I really have no idea what to say about all of this."

And then he smiled a bit, which felt odd given the conversation. "You could say that you don't believe me, Miss Fleming, that perhaps you believe I've lost my mind."

It felt somewhat jarring to hear him voice this, though she agreed. She could say all those things but didn't because it wasn't true. It was odd how all of this hit her, as though there was something about it that she'd forgotten and should remember but did not.

And then she'd left. It was rude, particularly with how candid he'd been with her. But she couldn't help it. She couldn't sort it out, any of it. She'd just excused herself rather abruptly, awkwardly, claiming a prior appointment. And then afterward, she'd sat in her room feeling as though her insides were shaking.

Meeting him, talking to him, Malachi McKellan had shaken her. And now it felt acutely as though her world had been somehow altered and left in disarray, though even that feeling made no sense.

She thought about checking out immediately, cutting this untenable experiment of hers short. But she didn't. Instead, she lay down on the bed, closing her eyes in fatigue. And that was when, almost immediately, she began to dream.

There was exhaustion and heat coming from inside her as though she were burning up internally. It was difficult to breathe, so hard to draw air in. Darkness was everywhere. The night was cool, but the heat within was excoriating. She dragged herself across the smooth stone surface of the courtyard. Everything was silent except for music, distant music drifting in from the outside city streets.

The pain struck again, so intense that her slippered feet stumbled across the stone, the long heavy silk gown twisting about her ankles as she fell, her head hitting hard as it collided, cracking against the cold stone surface.

"Step back," whispering in her mind, "You're too close." The pain exploded everywhere from the impact. She could barely see the figure as it walked out of the house, the tall, dark shadow moving toward her. But the scream, her scream, was without volume, trapped in her throat.

"Josie!" It was loud, a jarring command ripping through her. She jolted up in the bed. The room was dark, the ceramic ceiling fan slowly turning above her. Shaking, she checked her watch, nearly seven. How long had she been asleep?

Abruptly, the phone next to the bed rang loudly, startling her. She stared at it for a moment in confusion, complete confusion as it repeatedly went off. Her hands were actually trembling as she picked up the receiver as much to make it stop as anything else. "Yes," in a near whisper.

"Miss Fleming, this is Malachi McKellan." She took a deep breath but found it was still difficult, just as in the dream. The feeling was still with her, in her limbs, paralyzed out there, lying on the cold stone of the courtyard. "Are you all right?"

The voice was strong and intense, managing to yank her out of the fog she was trapped in. "Yes, I—I was asleep. What is it, Mr. McKellan?"

There was a long pause at the other end, then "I was wondering if you would have dinner with me tonight. There are things I'd like to talk to you about."

It took a moment to sink in. "Dinner?" still struggling with confusion.

"Yes, I can meet you at your room in fifteen minutes unless you need more time." Her head was spinning. She wasn't exactly sure what was going on. "Josie," he said softly. "It's important."

She hesitated, having no idea how to respond. "Yes, okay," she murmured, not at all sure if this was wise.

"Good," and then he hung up.

She continued to sit there for a moment, a bit dumbfounded, just staring at the rose-colored phone receiver in her hand.

"Is this all right?" he asked.

She looked up from the menu with distraction. "Yes, it's fine." They'd chosen Maspero's, a popular spot on Royal St. that served typical New Orleans fare — po'boys, seafood, jambalaya, and of course, gumbo. But Josie was still finding it difficult to focus on much of anything.

Malachi reached across the small corner table, touching her hand as though in response to her distress. And it startled her. There had been very little conversation once he'd arrived at her room. She'd only had moments to straighten her hair a bit and put on some lipstick before it seemed he was at her door. Then it had been. "Are you ready to go? Do you mind walking?" Everything seemed to be in a rush, designed to get them moving with very little time to consider much of anything. And now they were sitting at a corner table at this well-populated French Quarter restaurant, and Malachi McKellan had his hand over hers as though now they were on a more personal footing. "Are you all right, Josie?" he asked.

She took in a breath. "I—I have no idea."

Then he smiled. It was a nice smile, warm and familiar, comforting perhaps. "Maybe some food will help. But you'll have to help me. I'm not indigenous to this area."

He'd removed his hand, but her skin still tingled from where he'd touched her. It dawned on her distantly that this, indeed, was attraction. She was drawn to him on that level, in a physical way. Maybe it was slow to penetrate because they'd known each other so briefly, and she, at present, was feeling completely scrambled. "Something simple, maybe a shrimp po'boy and a beer."

"Now that sounds perfect."

"What's happening?" she murmured for no real reason except that she felt she didn't have the power not to say it.

"Let's eat and relax. Then we'll talk, all right?"

She nodded slowly, "But you know, don't you?"

"Some, I know some."

Eating did help. She felt a bit more grounded, and then there was coffee and bread pudding for dessert. He was from Colorado, at least that was where he lived now, though he'd said he'd lived all over the country.

"So why did you pick the Bienville?" he asked, a bit out of nowhere.

They were just finishing their coffee when the question came up. "Oh, honestly, it's hard to say. There are a lot of interesting niche hotels in New Orleans as well as a whole host of bed-and-breakfast inns. I guess it was more of a feeling than anything that drew me. The mystery of it, I suppose."

"Because of its reputation?"

"Partly, and—" she stopped.

"And?" he prodded, though waiting for her to gather her thoughts.

"I don't know how to express it. I was just drawn there." He nodded in acknowledgment as though that made perfect sense. He seemed to understand, even if she didn't. "You said it was a complicated place you believed was haunted."

"Yes, I did. There are layers of paranormal phenomena there."

"Is that why you're here?" she asked, "To write about it?"

He leaned back in his chair, his eyes fixed solely on her. "Not exactly, Josie. I'm here because of you."

Her eyes widened in shock. "Because of, did you say because of me?"

"Yes, there is a danger for you there. I think you felt that today."

"No, I have no idea what you're talking about."

"The dream," he said slowly. "The woman in the courtyard, you were experiencing her trauma."

"How, how could you possibly know about that?"

"Because I pulled you away from it." He said it so calmly, matter of fact, as though it was not the extraordinary statement that it was.

"The voice I heard," she whispered, not at all sure if it was even voiced.

"Yes," he said. "You must understand how sensitive you are, Josie, and unfortunately vulnerable as well. The ghost drained you greatly."

"What, what does that mean, drained me?"

"Of energy, it was using you like a battery for itself."

She stared at him almost in disbelief, almost, but he just sat there as though what he was saying was completely factual, not fantastical in the least. "Mr. McKellan."

"Malachi, please, I think we've moved a bit beyond formality."

"I don't understand at all what you're saying to me. But on the outside chance that any of this is true, all I need to do is leave, go home."

"Yes, that would seem the simplest solution. Unfortunately, now it's not that easy. The spirit in question, the lost one, has managed to form a bond, a link if you will, that we need to disengage you from. It happened quickly, more quickly than I expected. We, you and I, need to find a way to break it."

She shook her head slowly in the last whimper of denial. Because she did believe him, she had no idea why, but she did. "This sounds like madness."

"I can see why you'd think so, but you need to trust me, Josie, so I can help you. And we don't have time to waste."

Three months earlier

"I've seen her again."

"Ah, The Woman," Simon murmured.

Malachi turned to respond to the change of tone in Simon Tull's voice. He'd come to use the term "The Woman" as it was used for the character of Irene Adler in Sir Arthur Conan Doyle's "A Scandal in Bohemia." In that particular story, Sherlock Holmes had a special designation for only one noteworthy woman he'd encountered. Malachi's spirit guide had gotten in the habit of referencing this particular female as "The Woman," though exactly why Malachi had yet to root out. "It was in a dream last night. She was at that strange hotel again, traveling there in her astral body."

"The one in New Orleans?" Simon was leaning against the cottage wall, smoking his ornately carved cherry wood pipe. Malachi would have told him not to smoke, except that the cottage wasn't exactly physical but rather one that existed deep within Malachi's subconscious. In addition, Simon Tull was an English fellow who had lived and died several centuries before, so second-hand smoke could hardly be an issue under the circumstances.

"Yes, every week or so, I continue to be drawn into her dream state or find myself near her when I'm in a deep meditation. I can't really account for it."

"It's a spiritual connection. You two have something to do together."

Malachi sighed. He found it perplexing. In his thirty years on the earth, he had never experienced anything quite like this, although it was undeniable that he had seen quite a bit. "This draw she has to this place is concerning. It's as though something or someone is luring her there."

Simon took a puff on his pipe and then lowered it as though he were considering for a moment. "Can you pinpoint the place, the particular hotel?"

"I haven't been able to yet."

"You might need to. And definitely keep an eye on the situation. The Woman, does she have a name yet, Malachi?"

"Yes, her name is Josephine."

"I see," Simon replied quietly before he moved on to other matters.

They left the restaurant, moving into the darkness of the night, although the street was quite well lit. "We need to talk some more, Josie."

She was silent beside him as they slowly walked back to the hotel. She battled the conflict within her. Her head was swirling in confusion. Her mind argued that she shouldn't give any credence to what she'd been told, simply reject his assertions as the ravings of someone who could be quite possibly unhinged. But her senses, her emotions, argued something else. And there was that dream, so disturbing, painfully vivid that had undeniably taken so much out of her. "I imagine this is a lot for you to take in," he murmured.

"Yes, I have no idea what to think," she answered, her voice hollow, feeling a bit gutted on the whole.

"And yet you haven't run for dear life, so I gather you haven't completely dismissed what I've told you."

"I, I don't know why, but I can't."

He slipped his hand into hers as they walked. "Yes, well, the truth is like that, very difficult to just ignore when you hear it."

As they returned to the Bienville, Malachi felt extremely concerned. There were strange, unnatural energies all over Josie Fleming, as though something had reached out and was trying to take control of her. He'd considered moving her somewhere else, far away from the walls of the Bienville, but at present, it seemed more prudent to confront the matter head-on at its source.

He had felt the alien energy progressively increase. The closer the proximity to the hotel on Royal St., the more of a drain he could feel on her. Something was actively pulling the energy out of her. He knew the action could be misinterpreted, but he wrapped his arm around her, firmly pulling her against him in a protective stance.

"Where are we going?" she whispered as they passed the entrance to her room in the courtyard.

"My room," he said flatly.

"I don't feel well. Something is wrong."

"It's all right." He continued concentrating on surrounding her with protective energy to countereffect the drain.

As they stopped in front of the French doors leading to his room, she murmured, "I don't understand why you're doing this." But he didn't answer because that was another matter completely.

Once they were in the room, he insisted Josie lie down. He could see clearly that her aura had been significantly diminished by the attack through the dream. While she rested, Malachi slowly paced, considering. He'd been at the Bienville since the middle of the week and had examined several options to contain the primary problem here. He and Simon had already taken more than one astral journey in hopes of freeing some of the trapped souls at the Bienville but to no avail.

"The strongest entity is very old and strong," Simon explained. "But it needs energy, a particular sort of energy."

"Particular?"

"Yes, the creative kind, empathic kind."

"Josephine?"

"Possibly, if we could dissuade her from coming here."

"I've tried, on more than one occasion, to plant deterrents in her mind as she slept, but they always seem to get overridden."

Simon had nodded. "Yes, well, perhaps it's a spiritual path that she goes to the Bienville. If that is so, there must be some real purpose for her being there."

She had fallen into a light sleep that felt troubled as she stirred often. He'd remained close to her, trying to prevent her astral self from traveling into another precarious journey. He'd felt her intense sensitivities as she'd approached his table out in the courtyard earlier in the afternoon. He'd actually encouraged the contact, sending out energy to lure her in a bit. That was often easy to do with people who weren't paying attention to what they were really feeling and why. Most people sort of sleepwalked through this aspect of their lives, though everyone did have the innate ability to be more cognizant of such things.

Of course, he'd been aware of her for some time — The Woman — as Simon referred to her. The contacts had started nearly a year ago. He could tangibly feel a pull when she was upset or focused intensely on something. In doing so, she had reached a certain energy vibration that resonated with him. And beyond everything, there had been the familiarity. He knew her, knew her spirit. She had undoubtedly been a significant person to him in other lives when they had been very close. Simon, who was curiously silent on the matter, didn't have to tell him this. It was more than clear.

And then they'd met, physically, in the flesh, and all those impressions came rushing back to him as well as new ones. There was a tangible and obvious awareness now of how very drawn and attracted he was to her in this life.

Her eyes flickered open, and she began to sit up. "Malachi," she nearly whispered. He was by her side, instinctively taking her hand in his.

"I'm here," he said with comfort.

"There's a woman dressed in clothes from long ago. I keep seeing her clearly standing out in the courtyard. She feels as though I should know her."

He nodded, "Yes, that is Amelie Chenier. She owns this place."

Josie rubbed her eyes. She could still clearly see the image in her mind. A petite woman with dark curly hair that framed her pale face and eyes, so dark they could almost be black. "What does that mean, owns this place?"

He was sitting beside her on the bed, holding her hand. It felt stabilizing in a way, his skin touching hers. Amid all the craziness that was happening, this fact was slowly penetrating the fog that was around her mind.

"From what I can put together, there is a hierarchy of ghosts, though I prefer to call them lost souls, who are trapped in the earthly plane on the grounds of the Bienville. The woman, Amelie Chenier, appears to be a sort of hybrid. She died traumatically in the 1700s, was murdered by an unfaithful husband, and perished in such a heightened state of horror and vitriolic anger that it drew an entity to her that had been preying on her while she was alive. The very soil and structures within and around the Bienville are permeated with a very low and negative energy that draws creatures of a similar frequency. Amelie, being so vulnerable, ostensibly merged with a low one upon her death. Through her, it has drained many people over the centuries, people who have lived here, and in the present patrons or employees of the hotel."

Her mind was reeling from what he was telling her. "How do you know this? Are you a psychic?"

He squeezed her hand. "We're all psychic, Josie. It's just a matter if we decide to develop those latent abilities. But you could say that I do study the paranormal."

"You said people who are vulnerable."

"Yes, my sister is what you would call a profound empath. This predisposition makes her vulnerable to certain types of spiritual attacks, at times spiritual draining. I believe you may have a similar predisposition."

"So, you believe this Amelie, or whoever she is, has been draining me."

"Yes, unfortunately, I'm certain of it."

She abruptly pulled her hand away, swinging her legs back down to the hardwood floor of the room. Her head swam with dizziness. Breathing heavily, she tried to get her bearings. "All right," she rasped a bit. "All of this, what you're saying, sounds so bizarre. But what can we do?"

He stood up, walking across the floor. "Permanently here? I'm not really sure that anything can be done. This place is toxic, but we must sever the connection you now have with Amelie."

"And how do we do that?"

"I've been keeping her away from you while you slept. I think it might just be time to let her in."

She couldn't help but wonder if she'd even heard him right. "That sounds like a terrible idea."

"No, not really, because you won't be alone."

"I'm nervous. I'm not sure I can relax enough to go to sleep."

"Don't worry, just close your eyes and try to drift."

It was true. She was unbelievably exhausted, and sleeping now really wouldn't be a problem, but she was also afraid, so afraid that somehow, she wouldn't come back from this. "Malachi, what if something goes wrong?"

His voice came soothingly from across the room. "I'm not going to let anything happen to you, Josie, trust me." And in the next moment, she allowed herself to relax and let go, let go and be pulled deeply into a heavy slumber.

The awareness that she was dreaming was distant, tucked away somewhere apart. But she was moving, moving forward toward the main house where the doors lay open, and the oil lamps illuminated the inside. She paused, looking around. There was such a pull, a tremendous pull to go within, but she actively tried to resist it. "What are you feeling?"

The courtyard was only illuminated by moonlight and the glow from the main house's interior, but she could now see Malachi standing next to her. "How did you—"

"It's all right. You're connected to her, Josie. What does she want?"

"She wants me inside. I can feel it, so strong."

"It's all right. Resist as you've been doing. It would be symbolic of a total merge."

"Merge? What does that mean?"

"She's been working toward that a long time, amassing energy so that she can actually merge with a living person. That was what she attempted the other night in the dream."

"Do you mean possession?"

"Of a fashion, now I want you to focus and completely embed yourself here so she must come to you. I am helping you, Josie."

It was difficult, so incredibly difficult. She could feel emotions, tendrils of emotions wrapping around her, anguish, upset, fear, trying to convince her that they were indeed hers. But with Malachi next to her, she could separate a bit and understand that these feelings did not belong to her. She focused deeply on being rooted, completely rooted to where she was.

Within, there was movement. She could see it near the open French doors leading out onto the courtyard, a fluttering of the white cotton drapes covering them. And then Josie felt a lurch inside her as though something was forcefully ripping at her. It was profound, a pain right through her ribs. "It's all right, Josie. Ground yourself." He was behind her now. His hands were on her shoulders as he pulled her against him in an embrace. She could feel his strength pouring into her as the pain lessened.

Without warning, the doors flew suddenly open, pulled fiercely apart, and the woman walked out onto the courtyard. Josie felt as though all breath had left her body. Amelie was standing there in a long black velvet dress with her dark hair piled up high on her head and her eyes blazing distinctly red. "She's so strong," she whispered.

"Not stronger than you are," he murmured into her ear, still holding her against him.

The woman outstretched her hands toward her, speaking in French, "Venez à moi."

Josie could hear it so loud, in her mind, in her skin. "Malachi!"

"I know. Focus on breaking the link Josie, focus."

She did as he asked with all her might, envisioning a complete separation from the woman trying to pull Josie's essence toward her. And then somewhere, and she suspected it largely came from Malachi, she could feel a fierce tearing inside her, an actual physical ripping. And in her mind, next to her, everywhere, a shrill scream, frantic yet enraged, pierced the air. Then complete silence, she breathed in deeply, feeling acutely as though something tangible had been pulled out of her. Unable to do anything else, she collapsed backward into his arms.

Josie awoke jarringly, trembling all over and feeling distinctly as though she had just run an incredible distance. Malachi, sitting next to her, looked at that moment just as bad as she felt. He reached out his hand softly, touching her cheek. "I'm going to get you out of here."

Lucy seemed more than a bit befuddled when Josie returned to their apartment close to midnight with a man she had never seen before. Equally peculiar was the fact that Josie had invited him to spend the night on their sofa.

"I just dropped you off this afternoon, and now you're bringing home a stranger. What happened to your story? You were supposed to stay until Sunday."

Josie assured her that once they all got some sleep, she would explain everything, which translated into until she could think of a decent cover story for all of this. At the Bienville, Malachi had insisted they call a cab, and she clear out that night. And she, in turn, had insisted he not return there, at least that night as well, thus the couch. The next day he was up by six, insisting that there was unfinished business for him there, something about trying to help the other ghostly residents that Amelie was suppressing. Also, he needed to put in safeguards to somewhat reduce her influence. He seemed focused, all businesslike, given their recent closeness, and she wondered dubiously if she would see him again.

But late that afternoon, he called asking to take her out to dinner. She met him at Fitzgerald's, a restaurant on the lakefront. "What did you tell Lucy?" he'd asked. She could tell by the tired look in his eyes what a toll all of this was taking on him. He was sitting across from her at a secluded table near a plate glass window with a direct view of Lake Pontchartrain.

"Not too much, that we'd met at the hotel, hit it off, and that there was an air conditioning problem with your room they needed to fix last night. Pretty thin, but she seemed to accept it somewhat." He nodded, seeming a bit lost in thought. "Malachi, I'm worried about you. I mean, still being at that place."

He looked up with an odd expression. "I'm not. I checked out and into another hotel downtown. Look, it's best you avoid the French Quarter for the time being, Josie, at least until you recover a bit and things settle down."

"And are they settling down?"

"To a degree, Simon and I have been doing as much damage control as possible. I think we've made some impact."

"Who's Simon?" she asked.

"Oh," he said, stirring a long spoon around in his iced tea. "He's a friend who's helping me."

"Do I get to meet him?"

He looked back at her, smiling a bit. "Maybe, sometime," he said a bit evasively. And she was a reporter, so she could spot evasiveness a mile away.

"You're very mysterious, Mr. McKellan," she said softly.

"Not really, Miss Fleming," he replied, "if you get to know me."

Malachi was only supposed to spend a week in New Orleans, but he stayed a month and then rented half of a double off of City Park Avenue. At that point, he moved to the city permanently, and in the next year, they were married. And in their years together, Josie managed to unravel quite a few of his mysteries.

Between

"I don't really understand why they're so upset."

"It's grief and fear."

"Yes, but I'm fine. I feel better than ever."

"They don't realize this. All they know is that you are very ill, becoming more incapacitated." The old man glanced back to the hospital bed, looking a bit confused. Malachi could clearly see the light diaphanous spray of golden web connecting the elderly fellow to his slumbering physical self. When Malachi first stumbled upon him outside his room, he started bemoaning the upset state of the visitors he'd been receiving as of late.

"I forgot about that," the man muttered, staring at his essentially inert body lying so very still.

"It's all right," Malachi murmured, trying to comfort. "That's normal."

It was normal for a spirit ostensibly in between, not yet having left their earthly body but not quite still in it either. But as Simon Tull had schooled him on more than one occasion, there was a time of death, a fixed time of departure, and until that happened, we were still somewhat attached to our mortal coil.

The old man circled the room lightly, scarcely resembling the motionless body. "I feel things pulling me elsewhere."

"Yes, that's normal too. Your senses aren't restricted the way they are when, well, the way they used to be."

He didn't want to say exactly the way they were when you were in your body. From what he understood, once someone crossed the veil, there would be an education period about the true nature of things. But someone in this in-between state was vulnerable in many respects — one foot in, one foot out. And the last thing he wanted to do was upset him.

"A little surprised to see you here, Malachi." He glanced up at Simon Tull, now standing in the doorway.

The old man's eyes widened at the sudden appearance of Malachi's spirit guide, all decked out in his nineteenth-century garb. "Who is that?"

"This is Simon Tull, a friend of mine. Simon, this is Samuel."

He tilted his head in the old man's direction. "Samuel, it a pleasure to make your acquaintance," he responded in his rich British accent.

The old man looked even more confused at the further intrusion. "Simon, perhaps we should move on and allow Samuel to get his bearings. It probably would be a good idea to rest a bit my friend."

Again, Samuel's eyes flickered over the motionless body in the hospital bed. "Back there?"

Malachi again attempted to sound comforting. It was a delicate time for this fellow. "Just for a bit, don't worry. Things will sort themselves out before very long."

And in the next instant of thought, he and Simon Tull were standing in the hallway of St. Anne's Convalescent Home on Carrollton Avenue. The lights were dim down the long cold stretch, but while it should have been silent, Malachi could clearly see much activity. Many others, in addition to Samuel, were out and about roaming these halls at night, in and out of their bodies, testing the boundaries. "You know spending too much time here can be draining to someone like you. There are so many in great need."

"I know," Malachi murmured, feeling the energy depletion in his chest. "But I was called here."

"Called? By Samuel?"

"No, no, I don't think so. I haven't been able to pinpoint it, but I felt a profound pull to this place when I meditated this morning. I ignored it for a while but then decided to investigate."

"Well, that's vague. Any idea where to begin?"

Malachi smiled, "No, actually, none whatsoever."

"Would you rather I leave?" Simon asked.

"No," Malachi said softly. He stilled for a moment, trying to separate himself from the commotion he felt from the residents of St. Anne's traveling about throughout the facility. He was interested in one voice, one particular voice that had been strong enough to reach out to him. And then his perception shifted a bit. Quite suddenly, at the end of the long hall, he saw a figure, a young woman with red hair watching him intently. But what was odd about her was that she was dressed in a long gown that reached down to the floor, costumed in garb from clearly another time.

"Now that one is definitely not like the others," Simon murmured a bit dryly. And then, quite hurriedly, she turned and walked out of sight.

In the next moment, without thought or consideration but instinctually, Malachi followed her. It was the pull, a strong, undeniable pull that he felt from the woman. He didn't stop to see if Simon was with him because, in some respects, this felt desperate. Instead of the usual movement he experienced when he was in the astral state, he distinctly now felt as though he was running, oddly running in a bit of panic after her.

Rather quickly, he found himself in the doorway of a corner room. His chest felt quite decidedly as though it were caving inward from the exertion, though that really didn't make any sense. There wasn't usually physical exertion in the astral state. But here he found her, the woman with the red hair, standing next to a patient's bed. It was an elderly lady asleep that she watched, one with an IV tube hooked up to her arm.

The girl, because in looking at her closely, he could say that she might only be in her late teens, just stood there, motionless, raptly staring at the sleeping form. She was dressed as he'd seen her before in the long off-white gown made of heavy fabric. Wool entered his mind, though why exactly he couldn't say. It was well fitted to her slight form, having small black buttons running from the simple collar down to the waist. So odd, her garb, her posture, why did it all feel so familiar?

"Charles," her voice was strong, rich in tone, though she was so young. "Do you see how he sleeps so serenely?"

He glanced back to the bed. That didn't make sense. Clearly, there was a woman in the bed, an old woman, though the girl saw something else. Then suddenly, he felt a punch in his chest, a loss of energy.

"My name is Malachi McKellan."

Then she looked at him warmly, eyes sky blue. "Don't be foolish. You're my Charlie, my little brother. Look," she said, gesturing to the old woman on the bed. "I've found him again," then she smiled, chilling him, "I'll never let him escape."

"What did you feel from her?"

"Familiarity, as though I should know her."

Simon continued to pace across the pinewood floor of Malachi's mountainside cabin, the cabin that existed somewhere deep in the recesses of Malachi's subconscious. "It was odd the way you responded to her, almost like an embedded memory. You actually tore down the hall in a sort of panic, very strange."

Malachi agreed. It was strange, all of it. He wasn't accustomed to losing control like that, but he had. "Yes, she said I was her little brother Charles, Charlie, and that she'd found him, though the him was a her, an old woman, a patient at St. Anne's. What in the world could all of this mean?"

Then Simon stopped and eyed Malachi a little grimly. "The question is, what do you think it means, Malachi?"

He grimaced, tired and struggling against a measure of irritation. "I have to tell you, my friend, that I am not at all in the mood for psychological games."

"It's certainly not a game," Simon replied. "It's clear you have more answers than you think. Consider deeply, what is your feeling about all of this?"

Malachi abruptly stood up from the couch, and Nuance growled in response. Clearly, she'd just gotten comfortable. It felt aggravating, all of it, but he forced himself to summon the image of the young woman in his mind.

Quite strongly, he could see her face again, her great cornflower blue eyes and carrot top, red hair. And there had been freckles sprinkled somewhat sparsely around her nose, actually quite the lovely picture. He focused more intently, seeing her sitting outside, on the grass somewhere, laughing full-heartedly, fiercely, and then the whole memory became pain. All of it felt like sheets of acute torment to him. "You do know her," Simon whispered.

Malachi moved to the fireplace, crouching down and staring into the mutating flames. "Yes, it seems so. It feels like a past life, but it's incredibly difficult."

"Traumatic?" Simon murmured.

Malachi struggled to clear his mind and let the images float in unrestricted. He could see it, another place, but he was young, so much younger, not even a teenager yet. And everywhere, all around, there was sobbing, crying, anguish — people in terrible grief, mourning. He yanked back, breathing deeply. The emotions were so raw. "It's very hard," he mumbled. "A death," the words seemed caught in his young throat, but no, he wasn't young. He was a sixty-five-year-old man in the United States, not that other place.

"The girl?" Simon pressed.

He forced himself back, slipping into that other time, the girl with the blue eyes, his sister. "You must find that bastard. He beat her, cut at her. My poor girl, my poor—"

"Davan," Malachi whispered with genuine anguish. He understood now. His father had been the one talking. He could still hear the heavy timbre of devastation in his words.

"I see," Simon said softly.

"She was murdered horribly. He beat her, then stabbed her."

"And yet she was at St. Anne's."

Malachi nodded gravely, the dark realization of what was happening floating over him. "She said she'd found him again. She can't. I mean, she must have moved on, crossed over. I would have known it surely."

Simon sighed deeply, "Perhaps not. There is a timing in everything. For Davan, it's possible that where she is feels as though no time has passed at all, but for you perhaps centuries. She is caught up, it appears, in a self-proclaimed mission."

"Tracking her murderer?" Malachi asked.

"Wreaking vengeance, my friend, perhaps the eternal kind."

There is always choice involved in pretty much everything. Even at times when one feels as though there is no choice in a situation, the choice is in how to react, what emotion to allow to govern. And even at that moment of death, there is choice. At times the majority and at other times, a smaller percentage choose to cross into their new life, while others choose, whether consciously or reactively, not to do so. Without choice, no one would evolve or devolve as it were.

Malachi considered deeply what was to be done here. There was emotion in it for him. Strong feelings and attachment carried over from a past life. In this life, he was not Davan's brother but the remembrance, the remembrance of caring, bore with it a feeling of obligation. She'd gotten lost. What had happened to her, its traumatic nature, was not her fault, but her choices as a consequence were indeed a different matter. It had become clear to him that somehow if she was in any way reachable, he needed to make her understand this truth.

He spent the following day recharging, walking outside, and spending time in an empty cathedral. As a place of worship, a church was most often filled with positive energy. The good intentions and good thoughts of its parishioners, regardless of denomination, seeped into and permeated the building. He did add usually, however, because there were always exceptions. If a place of worship were turned into a negative experience, as if tainted by those preaching exclusion and attack, then the emotions and energy of the structure would invariably turn negative.

Malachi spent this time rebuilding himself and erecting barriers of calmness so that he could be of substantive help when the time came. Simon had taught him early on that you could be of no aid to others if you didn't first care for yourself. He wasn't certain if it was his reticence to return to St. Anne's or a real need for extra preparation. Still, he ended up taking several days before he attempted a meditation in which he would engage Davan.

"Do you want me to go with you?"

"No, I think I'd better do this alone."

"Are you sure?"

"No, not at all, but I will try."

Simon agreed and continued to smoke his cherry wood pipe. Nuance nuzzled Malachi's side, and he understood suddenly that he was actually very much dreading this encounter. His chance of success was low at best. And he had no idea if the girl who once was his sister could really be reached in the state that she existed in. Spending time between realities did tend to take its toll.

The very last thing he did in preparation was once again to pay a visit to St. Anne's Convalescent Home, not as he had before. He did not go in an astral state but rather in the flesh. When he arrived in the old woman's room, the one whose former life had been lived as his sister's murderer, it was empty, empty of visitors and of Davan as well. This was fortunate because he wanted to spend a little time alone with this patient, time enough to gather ammunition.

Malachi felt the need for a neutral space. He visualized a calm place, a picturesque creek situated in a lush, enchanting forest. He spent time constructing the details in his mind. There was lovely green grass, as he remembered her sitting on from memory, and tall trees overarching, filtering the direct sunlight. And, of course, the water, which was profoundly important, there must be an entrancing, hypnotic sound to the water that soothed the emotions. They needed calm. He needed calm in order to try to reason with Davan in her unstable state of mind.

He placed himself there, visualizing in his mind. Then once the scene was firmly established, his astral self followed. Breathing deeply and bringing his consciousness up to the highest level of serenity he could achieve, he opened himself to their connection. Ostensibly, he called her.

One not committed to a stable form of existence was easily influenced. They were not tied down to anything in particular, which, while it might sound appealing in some respects, was actually quite a hardship. It caused confusion in the mind, disorientation, and at times great depression. It is not unlike a person who feels their entire life has no meaning or purpose. They live in a constant state of angst and with an extreme loss of energy which is nearly impossible to replenish.

Grounding himself with all the energy he'd gained over the last several days, Malachi doubled down on bringing Davan to him. And after quite some time, he opened his eyes to find her standing before him.

It startled him at first. Of course, he should have expected this. Those who were so disconnected often clung to something representing a powerful emotion remembered from their last life. In Davan's case, it was her murder. She stood before him in the same off-white wool dress he'd seen her in at St. Anne's, but now the garment was drenched. Blood gushed from the stab wounds her former sweetheart inflicted on her. She stood before him, literally dripping from the wounds that had not dried but were still flowing freely.

The horror and emotion from that past life surged within him at the sight. His first impulse was rage, profound anger, and then the desire to revenge himself on the man that had done this to his beloved sister. But then he stopped and forcibly stepped aside from those gut-level inclinations. This event had happened long ago, and the goal here must not be revenge. The goal was to help his sister's spirit, which was clearly in significant pain.

Centering himself, Malachi attempted to recapture his peaceful mindset.

"Why are we here, Charlie?" she asked softly. There was the slightest tinge of an Irish accent lacing her quiet words.

"I'm here to help you, Davan."

She smiled, walking towards him, her pale face alight with excitement. "I knew you would help me. I've found him again, Nolan, but he's barred from me. I can't reach him as I could before."

"Sit down, Davan," he gestured to a spot on the grass beside him.

"No, Charlie, we must hurry before he's lost again. He has to pay for what he's done."

"Please, Davan," he murmured, trying to blanket both of them with peacefulness, peacefulness, and sanity because, in truth, the baser emotions — anger, rage, jealousy, fear — were a form of insanity or imbalance of the mind. "Come, sit with me."

She wrapped her arms about her in a protective stance. He could feel her fear. Where she existed, she was always afraid. But she did come closer, and he could feel the tug at his heart area. That was the danger in this. Many lost souls, or ghosts, if you will, became natural drainers. They were so desperate for energy that they stole it from any living source that they could.

But in this instance, Malachi allowed it. He needed time, and allowing Davan to drain some of his energy might just afford him that. She sank down onto her knees in front of him. "All right, Charlie, just for a moment, but you must promise me then you will come to help me."

"Yes, I promise I will help you, Davan." He did so, because it wasn't really a lie. It was what he dearly hoped would come to pass.

She sat back on her legs, the bloodstained dress beneath her. He remembered when he was quite young, sitting with her outside their home. *"Now, Charlie,"* she'd laughed, *"I'll tell you a story, one about the fairies who live in the woods. You know if you're not watching, they'll come steal your soul. They can't help but steal everything,"* she'd laughed in that merry way of hers, the way that you could feel right inside your heart.

"Davan, I do want to help you," he said.

"Yes, I need your help. The first time, after Nolan hurt me, I could reach him. Whenever I was just near him, he would get very upset, and his dreams were a terrible torment. He almost seemed happy when Da caught up to him, and they hanged him out in the woods. He wasn't crying, but he said it was my fault. If I hadn't taken up with Benjamin, he wouldn't have done it. Think of that, Charlie, my fault for him beating me and cutting me with his hunting knife. My fault!"

Again, he tried to quell the vivid emotions rolling over him. It was essential that he maintain the calm. "Yes, Davan, what he did to you was horrible, but you can't let it destroy you."

She shook her head. He remembered that too, her tossing her long red hair. *"Don't be daft, Charlie!"* she'd say.

"No, no, Charlie, that's why I'm here to make him suffer for what he did. It was so hard looking for so long, then there he was. But I can't reach him. I don't understand."

"It's not him anymore, Davan."

"You don't see, do you?" He felt it again, that wrench in his chest that accompanied losing energy. She was pulling from him. She sprang to her feet, evidently invigorated by what she'd taken. "That's just as well. I'll do it myself," she nearly hissed. And at that moment, he was not reminded of his sister at all, but something else entirely, something more primitive that perhaps she was turning into.

Slowly, he stood up. There was a bit of disorientation in him from the energy that he'd lost. "No," he said haltingly. "I'll go with you."

It was difficult traveling in the realm where the lost ones existed. It was a punishing place for spirits to be in an unnatural space, cleaving to a life of the flesh distantly remembered but also existing in a realm of dissatisfaction. Essentially, they did not belong, and nothing could fill the void of being where one did not belong. All here was sadness.

They were at St. Anne's again, but it was different this time because he had consciously decided to sink himself into Davan's reality. Part of him wondered if he was incredibly foolish to be even trying this. Was this his place to try to help those that were so disconnected from everything he knew to be pure and real?

"And if you don't try? Then who will you be, Malachi?"

He remembered Josie's voice from long ago. She had always encouraged him to be the hero. But he never had felt the completeness of any sort of victory, not really. Living was much too complicated for such black-and-white evaluations. Losing her had taught him that. "Accept," you must learn to accept what is with no absolutes, no certainties, and simply remember the love.

They were in the room again of the old woman at St. Anne's. She was breathing lightly, but her spirit remained. Even in his diminished awareness, he could still feel that. It was a fact that, at times, the body did live longer than the spirit's occupation of it. The spirit might move on even though a body continued on life support or in a diminished capacity, lingering but near the end.

But this was not the case. The spirit who had once inhabited the lifetime of Nolan Buckley remained within this vessel, though quite dormant at the moment.

Davan again stood at the foot of the bed, but she'd forgotten the scars of her attack. She was as he'd seen her several nights before, in the same off-white woolen dress, red hair spilling across its simple construction. Though at the moment, her face screwed up in a grimace of frustration. "You see, Charlie. It isn't the same. He can't feel me here."

"It isn't him," he whispered. It was taking its toll. Perhaps he should have taken Simon with him, or, better yet, perhaps he should not have attempted this at all.

"What do you mean?" she rasped angrily. It was easy for her to be angry. On this plane of existence, the more base the emotions, the easier they were to slide into. He struggled to maintain some manner of higher thinking. "It is him. It is Nolan. I'm sure of it."

"No, it's not him, Davan. His spirit has reincarnated, but the man you knew as Nolan does not really exist anymore."

She turned toward him angrily. That was comfortable for her. "What foolery are you saying, Charlie?"

He braced himself. This was so much harder than he had anticipated. "The spirit comes to the earth to learn, Davan. Then it moves on to learn elsewhere. Nolan did something terrible to you, something that had consequences for his spirit. The universe balances actions and consequences. In order to evolve, he reincarnated as a woman, a woman who suffered great pain and abuse during her lifetime. It was important that he learn what he had inflicted."

She jerked her head again, facing the hospital bed with the old woman in it. Her eyes widened as though his words had somehow momentarily opened her to a new vision. "Aye, Charlie, I see. It is an old woman, but it is still Nolan, and it is my right to cause him pain."

He breathed in deeply. Things swirled. He could see things now around the room, lower things, creatures, feeding off the negative energy that had been created here. It was where she lived, and it pained him to see it. Beautiful, lovely Davan trapped in a hell of her own complicity. "No," he looked at her directly. "Davan, you are not God. You do not stand in judgment and take vengeance. Every spirit faces its own consequences for its behavior. You may not see it, but it is true. It has nothing to do with you. Both you and I have incarnated in past lives and have hurt people and have faced our own personal consequences. All of us will learn. Even those who seem the most culpable, the most depraved."

He held her eyes, those bluest eyes. And for a moment, he could feel their spirits touch as he imbued her with understanding. "But Charlie, what am I to do if not this?"

"Move on, Davan. Move on to a place where you are loved."

He felt a wave of dizziness and confusion. Then he felt himself yanked abruptly back into his own body. He was sitting in his den in a cross-legged position on the floor.

"*Enough*," he heard Simon's voice from somewhere. And then he said a prayer for Davan and quietly let her go.

"Do you want to work on the book tonight?" Simon asked.

Malachi shook his head. "Not yet, maybe tomorrow." They were sitting in his cabin. It had been several days since he'd traveled to help Davan. He hadn't asked for information about her. Somehow, he couldn't quite bear to hear what had happened to her for good or ill. Maybe at some point, but it all felt a bit too raw just now.

"Your friend, Samuel from St. Anne's, has moved on."

Malachi smiled. Now that was good news. The old man was more than ready. "Do send him my best wishes if you see him, will you, Simon?"

"Of course, my friend, of course."

The Wedding

"I'm very happy you made it, Malachi. I wasn't at all sure if you would."

He glanced up from the seat he'd taken against the wall. The reception hall itself was filled with round, brightly decorated tables as well as random seats placed along the perimeter, which he'd opted for as he'd traveled there alone. He'd even considered just going to the wedding somewhat anonymously and then sneaking back to his hotel. But something, curiosity perhaps, had urged him to stop by the reception of Evangeline's daughter, his niece Savannah.

Evie, the nickname he'd always used for her, sat beside him. She wore a lovely gown of a teal shade, her hair still blond but graying as was his. "You know, you could come and sit at the main table with the family."

"I didn't want to intrude, Evie," he murmured, feeling a little light-headed being in her proximity.

"So why did you? I mean, why come at all?"

He shrugged, "We're getting older. The future is less a certain thing than when we were young when we quarreled. And I thought it best to mend bridges."

His eyes were drawn to the beautiful young bride, with golden hair just like her mother, laughing and moving gracefully around on the dance floor with the tall, dark-haired groom. Already, he could see that the energy flowing from her into him was diminishing. It was two o'clock in the afternoon. By evening all the draining would have stopped.

One month earlier

"Perhaps you should go Malachi."

"To my niece's wedding? I haven't heard from Evie for over ten years. Our paths diverged a long time ago. She outright—"

"Yes, I know, rejected your life's calling."

"And hers, she was meant to be a remarkable empath, to use her gifts to help people."

Simon was perched on the stone hearth of the fireplace with one knee up and the other leg casually draped over the edge. Today, the fire wasn't lit. Sometimes when Malachi arrived at the cabin, it was lit. Sometimes it was flickering embers, and other times cold and untouched as it was today. He was sure this had a symbolic significance in his visualized refuge but, at present, hadn't unraveled it.

"Yes, and she chose a different course, a more conventional one with marriage and children."

"Ignored her spiritual path."

"You don't know that Malachi. No one really knows what another's preordained road is meant to be. All of that is fixed by the spirit."

He grumbled, "Yes, and why would she be so gifted if she were meant to ignore those gifts?"

"Perhaps to understand the price of ignoring them."

"And rejecting her brother in order to make her dim-witted husband happy."

"Hmm, carrying such a grudge, not very spiritual, is it?" Simon stood up, dusting off his tweed pants. "But it's not good for you, my friend, to hold onto anger for so long. You know that."

"It's not anger Simon. It never was. It was pain, all of that — the things that were said. Well, it's not easy to admit, but it hurt me deeply."

Simon nodded, "Of course, it did, my friend, but I recommend you consider this invitation. There may be more here than meets the eye."

"How's Tony?" he murmured, watching the trail of guests ebb and flow across the dance floor in the reception hall. His flight back to New Orleans was at five in the evening, so he didn't plan to stay very long at the gathering, just a little while to ensure things were falling into place.

"He's across the room if you'd like to say hello."

He leaned back in his chair. He didn't like it here. There were problematic sorts, a smattering of all types of individuals with energy spectrums that were disconcerting, to say the least. He glanced over at Evie sitting serenely beside him, wondering, having once been a highly sensitive empath, how she could stand it. But then again, he imagined the choices she'd made had probably caused her to retreat behind some sort of self-imposed shell just in order to survive. "No, I think his wedding present will be not having to speak to me."

She frowned just a bit, not enough for anyone else to notice but him. "You know, he's mellowed over time. He had a heart attack a few years back."

"I'm sorry to hear that."

"Are you Malachi? You acted as if you hated him at times."

"No, not hate. I just thought he was a poor choice of husband for you."

"It was never your choice to make."

"Yes, yes, you made that abundantly clear. But I wonder if he has really made you happy?"

She hesitated as though carefully framing her words. "We've made a life together. Both of us had to make concessions, adjust. Not everyone can have the love story you and Josie had."

"You know, I never wanted you to be unhappy. You made it clear that I wasn't welcome in your new life. But I suppose that's water under the bridge. And here is a new chapter—Savannah and Justin."

He watched her face as her eyes flickered over the bride and groom across the dance floor. And he saw it, though no one else would probably have noticed, a trembling in her chin, indecision in her eyes. She knew. She absolutely knew, and yet she'd told no one.

The month before

Malachi approved the final edits for his new volume on esoteric dream symbolism. He knew it was time to begin something new, but unfortunately, it was something old, something very old that occupied his attention.

"Anthony isn't like us. He believes your endeavors, your writings, are dangerous."

He might have laughed in her face. He wasn't sure, but at that time, the whole thing seemed ridiculous.

"Evie, you can't be serious. Why would you marry someone who is so alien to your nature?"

"Don't pretend you know what my nature is, Malachi. I want a home and a family, and Anthony can give that to me."

"But what do you have to sacrifice of yourself to get that?"

He breathed in deeply. He'd gone for a long morning walk along Bayou St. John, hoping the exertion would help clear his mind. But at present, all it had served to do was stir up a lot of old wounds. What was it that Simon would say? *"Wounds unaddressed eventually bleed all over everything,"* or something along those lines.

He continued to take long strides to the walking bridge that stretched across the bayou. At the moment, which was unusual, it was completely unoccupied. His shoes silently hit its metal construction, and the water beneath it glistened with the morning light reflecting artistically across its surface. But he was not soothed as he usually was. He'd been shocked when Evie had eloped, married her Anthony, and left everything else behind. They'd moved to Virginia, and then contact became sparse as though she deliberately wanted to keep her family of birth and her new family apart. He would see her once in a blue moon, especially as each of their parents became ill and then passed away. After that, the next time he heard from her directly was after Josie died. He hadn't bothered to let her know how serious the situation was until it was over. There was a card, and flowers sent that he didn't respond to.

And nothing again, until an invitation to a wedding, the wedding of a niece he'd only seen one or perhaps two times as a child. And something about it gnawed at him, something inexplicable.

He glanced one last time across the glistening water before he solemnly headed back to the house.

"Why in the world would she just run off like this?"

He remembered Josie had looked at him oddly as though what he was saying was a bit ludicrous. *"She fell in love with him, Malachi. I know you don't understand it.*

Maybe she doesn't even understand it, but it happened. And he is the one she wants."

He shook his head. *"All I can see is heartache for her."*

"Then that's her choice, and she'll have to live with it. Everyone has to live their own life. You remember the spirit's path of learning. Isn't that what you told me?"

He held the invitation in his hand, turning it over. There was something he felt from it, emotion, high emotion attached to it. Perhaps, it was simply the years of estrangement between the siblings. He sank onto the floor of his den and tried to clear his mind, tried to focus, which he found oddly difficult. But he modulated his breathing, visualizing his sister's face, Evie's face, as he remembered her. And he allowed himself to be pulled elsewhere.

The young woman resembled Evie around the eyes and had her coloring, but the rest of her came from parts unknown. He watched as she moved languidly through what he assumed was the den of her apartment.

It bothered him this place. Immediately, when he'd arrived, he'd felt a pronounced headache through his forehead. Perhaps, it was the familial connection, too painful to deal with.

"You're going to have to detach a bit, my friend, if you expect to figure this out." Simon stood beside him now, casually eying the woman who had settled on an off-white sofa. They watched pensively as she distractedly fiddled with her cell phone. "The niece, I presume."

"Yes, seems so," Malachi murmured. He didn't know if he really wanted Simon here. Actually, he didn't know if he really wanted to be here at all. Savannah leaned her head back on the sofa and closed her eyes.

"Is she ill?" Simon asked.

Malachi tried to focus, but it continued to be difficult. Then he shifted inward, changing his vision so that he could check her aura. He took a sharp breath inward. It was profoundly diminished. "Her energy is very low."

And in the very next moment, a man walked into the room. "Savannah," he nearly snapped. "We're meeting Ellen and Don for dinner. You need to get ready."

She sat up but still seemed extremely disoriented. "I'm feeling a little sick, Justin."

He took her hand and drew her to her feet. "Come on, lazy, I'll help you get dressed," he said, putting his arm around her. Malachi felt a lurch inside him at the sight. He could see the flood of blue-green energy just pouring out of Savannah into Justin.

"He's draining her," he whispered.

"Yes, seems to be the case," Simon murmured. "And they're living here together, which only makes it a thousand times worse. Well, at least they're getting married. That will solve one problem."

They'd quickly departed to Malachi's mountainside cabin to assess what little they could of the situation.

Malachi sat on the sofa with Nuance comfortingly curled up in his lap. "It's too bad the general population have disregarded the marriage ceremony as a worthless piece of paper."

"That has been a rather costly social aberration given the nature of its protective symbolism." Simon had explained to Malachi early on the powerful symbols inherent in the marriage ceremony, regardless of which religion or culture, which served to protect the participants, particularly when the match wasn't one properly suited to their spirits. In a nutshell, participating in the ceremony would completely stop the draining of Savannah by her fiancé.

"Yes, but this situation wouldn't occur if Savannah and Justin were actually a proper match."

"No, it couldn't. So, your niece will undoubtedly experience a difficult union. But you can't save her from that, free will and all, spiritual path and so on," Simon pronounced rather emphatically.

"In the old days, Evie would have seen this immediately and warned her daughter off."

"Well, that's a choice as well I suppose. I can't see that there's much to do here except hope they tie the knot sooner rather than later to stem the bleeding. No real need to attend the wedding unless it's something you want to do."

Malachi responded thoughtfully, "Yes, I suppose you're right."

"Please do let Savannah know I wish them every happiness," he murmured to Evie, who looked over to him a bit surprised.

"You're leaving?" she said softly.

"I am. This isn't my place," he said, standing up.

She followed him, a pensive look on her face. "Malachi, I read your last book. It was quite wonderful," she said softly, taking his hand.

"And what did Tony have to say about that?"

She smiled a little unexpectedly. "It wasn't really his business." He bent over and kissed his sister lightly on the cheek. "Stay in touch," she whispered.

He nodded and quietly left the celebration behind him.

Finis

More Books by Evelyn Klebert

Gravier's Bookshop
A New Orleans Paranormal Mystery (#1)
6 x 9 Softcover 190 pages
ISBN 978-1-61342-288-5

Caroline Breslin always knew that she would have to live her life differently. Being an extremely sensitive and gifted empath in a family full of psychics has led her to a somewhat cautious existence. But she is determined to strike out on her own, moving out of the protection of her Prytania Street home. And all is going well, except, of course, if you don't count the neighbor upstairs in her apartment building, who may or may not be a dark witch, and the increasing flow of malevolent energy that seems to be directed just her way. All of that and trying to make ends meet seems a bit much for this rather inexperienced New Orleans girl. The last thing Caroline wants to do is run back to her family for help, even though she is painfully in over her head. What she really needs is a knight in shining armor or maybe just that guy that keeps haunting her dreams.

Max Gravier had no intention of becoming a recluse, but after his wife's death, it seems his life is heading in that direction. He spends his time running Gravier's Bookshop on Magazine Street and occasionally, on the quiet, helps the police solve a crime with his psychic sensitivities. That is until he answers Caroline Breslin's call, a cry for help out of his dreams that draws him rather unexpectedly into a fierce battle for a young woman's soul. Join them and the whole Breslin family psychic clan in this first installment of The New Orleans

Paranormal Mystery Series, where you'll travel into a new world just a few steps into the turbulent realm of the unseen.

The Hotel Mandolin
A New Orleans Paranormal Mystery (#2)
6 x 9 Softcover 138 pages
ISBN 978-1-61342-290-8

Peril is wrapped up in the most enticing of disguises in *The Hotel Mandolin*, the second installment of The New Orleans Paranormal Mystery series. It's opulent, classic, and one of the most renowned hotels nestled deep in New Orleans' famous business district, but something is amiss at The Hotel Mandolin. PI Peter Norfleet is calling out the big guns to help him investigate a recent suicide at the famous establishment — his good friend Max Gravier, a formidable psychic, and his girlfriend, Caroline Breslin, a talented empath. But none of them can seem to scratch the surface of this puzzle, no one except Cassie Breslin, Caroline's clairvoyant mother, who has somehow tapped into an unexpected connection with a tragic ghost from the turn of the century. And the more she uncovers, the more dangerous and malevolent the mystery becomes.

More Books by Evelyn Klebert

The House at Pritchard Place
A New Orleans Paranormal Mystery (#3)
6 x 9 Softcover 136 pages
ISBN 978-1613422922

Nothing is really wrong with the old Warrick House on Dante St., except that there most certainly is. Nothing is exactly wrong with its new mysterious owner except that Elise is sure something doesn't add up. It isn't obvious, but sometimes the most dangerous things aren't. In the third installment of The New Orleans Paranormal Mystery series, with the help of her very psychic sister and her children, the Breslin clan, Elise Ashford is about to embark on a wild rescue mission straight into another dimension that will land her squarely somewhere she doesn't expect, right back into her past. She'll land full circle; in a childhood home whose memory still haunts her to this day — The House at Pritchard Place.

A Quiet Moment
6 x 9 Softcover 295 pages
ISBN 978-1-61342-326-4

Jacob Wyss is caught in a rut, in fact, on the verge of being engulfed by it. After an excruciating and disillusioning divorce, his life as an artist in a sleepy-college town at the foot of the Appalachian mountains has become quiet, routine, and maddening in its predictability. One wintry day, his deep restlessness drives him out in precarious conditions to a largely empty bookstore nearly devoid of another living soul, nearly.

Aimee Marston isn't like everyone else. On the surface, she lives a sedate life working as a feature writer for a small local newspaper in addition to several other editorial jobs to help make ends meet. But just beneath, her existence is largely not her own. She is a sensitive, an empathic psychic, guided by her calling to use her gifts to help others. Unfortunately, as a result, her secretiveness has made her defensive and protective of herself, preventing her from having much of a life.

A psychic call for help sends Aimee out on a freezing January morning, where her destiny and Jacob's collide, spiraling both their lives onto an unexpected and often disturbing track. Two lonely souls connect, not by accident, but by design. Theirs is the intersection of two spiritual paths, two lovers who must struggle to overcome the phantoms of a past life, as well as the challenges of their own inner demons to carve out an extraordinary future together.

More Books by Evelyn Klebert

Treading on Borrowed Time
6 x 9 Softcover 198 pages
ISBN 978-1-61342-214-4

For Julia Moreau, life seems complicated. Emerging from a failed marriage and managing a lifetime of diabetes, she lives alone in her childhood home, where she communicates with the spirit of her Great Aunt Lilia. But Julia doesn't have a clue what complicated is until she is thrust into being the key chess piece in a match between two powerful men of extraordinary abilities on the wild hunt for a mystical creature hidden in the heart of New Orleans' French Quarter. Will Julia lose her soul to the karma of a devastating past life or her heart to the love of a man driven by dark forces? What is clear is that whichever way she turns, she is *Treading on Borrowed Time.*

Sanctuary of Echoes
6 x 9 Softcover 338 pages
ISBN 978-1-61342-211-3

Ghosts unacknowledged do not sleep.

Corey Knight has resigned herself to a quiet, reclusive life spent living out the rest of her days in her childhood home on the fringes of New Orleans' French Quarter. But the unexpected specter of her deceased father plunges her into a mad quest for a missing supernatural weapon unearthed long ago. And unfortunately, her only ally is a lost love she once betrayed.

Iain Shaw returns to New Orleans, a city he abandoned a decade before while fleeing a devastating past. Here, he is forced to confront it again in the visage of the woman he once adored - one that he is now determined to get back at any cost.

Follow them both in a wild paranormal tale of discovery and redemption as they confront and unearth the echoes of a buried and unyielding truth that once tore them irreparably apart.

Dragonflies - Journeys into the Paranormal
6 x 9 Softcover 120 pages
ISBN 978-1-88756-072-6

A powerful wizard, love-crossed ghosts, a mysterious dark warrior, and an enigmatic time traveler -- a mystical wordsmith entices you into the world of the paranormal with a collection of inspired stories. Each tale takes the journey of the dragonfly imbued with the momentum and energy of change, following a winding path that will ultimately lead you to find the truth buried beneath perception.

A Ghost of a Chance
6 x 9 Softcover 174 pages
ISBN 978-1-88756-050-4

More Books by Evelyn Klebert

Jack Brennan, an ambitious high-powered attorney, dies, only to find himself constrained to a peculiar afterlife as an earth-bound spirit trapped in an old Virginia farmhouse with a very much living, reclusive writer of campy vampire novels. Hallie Barkly recovering from a painful and disillusioning divorce, has forged a career and exorcised her demons by writing under the pseudonym of Sebastian Winters. Their lives intersect, and two unconventional lovers are brought together under insurmountable circumstances. Together they must battle an unseen force hell-bent on possessing Hallie's life and bridge death itself to make possible what cannot be - to find a chance.

Breaking Through the Pale
6 x 9 Softcover 92 pages
ISBN 978-1-88756-045-0

Journey with metaphysical author Evelyn Klebert into a collection of short stories that travel beyond the pale into the unpredictable realm of the paranormal.
In "A Grey Mourning," a disillusioned man encounters a mysterious being on the foggy streets of New Orleans. "Contact" is a tale of automatic writing, when a young artist establishes communication with a spirit guide, and the victim of a car crash unravels the true nature of her existence in "Dancing on the Threshold." The final tale is called "Isolation," in which a confused and disoriented woman finds herself in an old, quaint house where she must piece together the mystical implications *surrounding her predicament.*

More Books by Evelyn Klebert

Explanations
6 x 9 Softcover 82 pages
ISBN 978-1-93493-515-6

In this, her second poetry collection, Evelyn Klebert takes us down the intricate path of a personal journey. Life, with its particular struggles, pitfalls, and ultimately triumphs, clearly begins to mirror a universal path, the quest for answers that we all ultimately pursue. In this reflective, esoteric collection, we can all explore and seek some of life's elemental mysteries and, hopefully, when all is said and done, emerge with some *Explanations.*

The Witches' Own
6 x 9 Softcover 124 pages
ISBN 978-1-61342-058-4

On the surface, things seem quiet and serene in the picturesque coastal village of Kilmarnock, Virginia. But something unseen roams its lush forests as the past and present collide, and the unthinkable begins to wreak its vengeance. Young Lucy Bonner is executed for witchcraft in the town's distant and brutal past. Her death triggers an unholy chain of events that grasp at the restless heart of novelist Peter McQuade, spurring him towards a quest to uncover the dark and terrifying truth.

The Left Palm
And Other Halloween Tales of the Supernatural
6 x 9 Softcover 104 pages
ISBN 978-1-93493-556-9

Halloween is the time of year when that veil between worlds is thinned, and you can just catch a quick glimpse into the realm of the unknowable. In this collection of short stories, Evelyn Klebert takes you to a place where ordinary life splinters into the sphere of the paranormal.

The journey begins with one woman's unstoppable quest for vengeance against a supernatural creature in "Wolves" and continues in an old historical graveyard where a horrifying discovery is uncovered in "Emma Fallon." In "The Soul Shredder," a psychiatrist's unusual patient opens his eyes to a disturbing new view of reality, while in "Wildflowers," a woman strikes up a supernatural friendship with impossible implications. And in "The Left Palm," a fortuneteller in the French Quarter receives a most unexpected and terrifying customer.

More Books by Evelyn Klebert

White Harbor Road
And Other Tales of Paranormal Romance
6 x 9 Softcover 130 pages
ISBN 978-1-61342-066-9

A psychic soul mate, a time traveler, a horror writer, and an enigmatic stranger take a selection of resilient, life-battered heroines to a place of paranormal healing and transformation. In this collection of short stories, White Harbor Road is the last stop where life's burdens and hardships evolve into something unexpected.

The Broken Vow
Vol. I of The Clandestine Exploits of a Werewolf
6 x 9 Softcover 140 pages
ISBN 978-1-61342-133-8

In the heart of every man, there is a history. In the heart of every monster, there is a story. In this first installment of *The Clandestine Exploits of a Werewolf*, Ethan Garraint is on a vendetta that begins in the heart of the Pyrenees with the fall of Montségur and leads him to the streets of New Orleans nearly five hundred years later. But the person he chases isn't really a man anymore, and Ethan has been a werewolf for almost a millennium. With the aid of a gifted seer, he is on a blood hunt that will culminate in a journey that crosses the line between heaven and earth and ends somewhere in between.

More Books by Evelyn Klebert

Travels into the Breach: Accounts of a Reclusive Mystic

6 x 9 Softcover 176 pages
ISBN 978-1-61342-323-3

At first glance, his life seems quiet, serene, and even uneventful. Malachi McKellan, a 65 five-year-old widower and author of esoteric books, lives largely as a recluse in a house situated just off the banks of Bayou St. John in New Orleans. But unbeknownst to most, he is also a bit of a detective, a specific kind of detective whose specialty is psychic attacks. Alongside his lifelong companion and spirit guide Simon Tull, a nineteenth century, twenty something English gent, Malachi battles the unseen, and is an unacknowledged hero to the most vulnerable - most of the population who have no idea what is really happening beneath the surface of the world in which they live.

In this collection of adventures, Malachi McKellan and Simon Tull wage war against the most insidious elements of the paranormal. In "The Three," Malachi and Simon come to the aid of a young woman being victimized by a group of dark witches. An old apartment building is the scene of an unimaginable battle against monstrous forces in "The Lost Soul." Malachi and Simon find themselves strategizing against a psychic vampire in "Obsession," and "The Hotel" turns back time to the 1980s where Malachi confronts a demonic spirit. In "Between," a past life is revisited as Malachi attempts to rescue a beloved sister from committing her existence to vengeance, and "The Wedding" takes a personal turn when Malachi must confront painful truths while endeavoring to protect his niece from a potentially devastating union. Travel into the Breach with a pair of paranormal warriors who choose to confront overwhelming forces on a battlefield unsuspected by most.

Considerations
6 x 9 Softcover 68 pages
ISBN 978-1-88756-062-7

Sometimes the struggle to understand the meaning and complexities of living comes down to a single moment of introspection or a fleeting yet meaningful reflection. This collection of poetry by Evelyn Klebert takes you down a winding path of self-discovery where the resolution may not always be absolute, but the journey is indeed unforgettable. It is a wide and varied map of inspired poetry for your examination and consideration.

Appointment with the Unknown: The Hotel Stories
6 x 9 Softcover 151 pages
ISBN 978-1613423608

A hotel, for most, represents a normal place, a predictable realm of commonality. One might even go as far to say a safe space, the reliable where nothing particularly unusual is expected to happen. Or is it? Dimensional traveling, spirit guides, mystical storms, and soul mates separated by time are only a few elements dotting this supernatural landscape. Drop into a collection of romantic paranormal stories where that place of commonality is only the threshold, the jumping-off point, for extraordinary adventures into the unknown.

The Tethering: A Portent of Crows
6 x 9 Softcover 201 pages
ISBN 978-1613425992

Deborah Brandt's beloved Aunt Gena always told her that she was special, a bit different, and would have to live her life, unlike other people. Of course, this she disregarded as the ramblings of her lovely but notably eccentric aunt. Although there were the things that Aunt Gena said that seemed true — like Deborah being sensitive to energy shifts, having potentially psychic impressions, and dreaming of a spirit guide — none of it could be real. But the most ridiculous thing that her Aunt Gena told her before she died was that someone special was out there for her. She said that he was an extraordinary man who was not only her perfect match but someone who she would learn from so that they could help the world in difficult times. How ridiculous! It sounds like a fairy tale, and no such person exists.

Daniel Wren is unique. He has been raised and trained from a young age to hone his psychic gifts. He lives in a world unimagined by most. And he has been waiting for years to contact his counterpart, soulmate, if you will. But the problem is that she is painfully unaware of the type of life that he lives and the life she would be entering into if they came together.

His dilemma becomes how best to proceed. How can he win her over and move forward before outside forces take that decision away from him?